19,20

D0929188

GAYLORD F

Sherlock Holmes and the Crosby Murder

SHERLOCK HOLMES
AND THE
CROSBY MURDER

A narrative believed to be from the pen of
John H. Watson MD

Edited and annotated for publication by
Barrie Roberts

CARROLL & GRAF PUBLISHERS
New York

Carroll & Graf Publishers
An imprint of Avalon Publishing Group, Inc.
161 William Street
New York
NY 10038 2607
www.carrollandgraf.com

First published in the UK by Constable,
an imprint of Constable & Robinson Ltd, 2001

First Carroll & Graf edition 2002

ISBN 0–7867–1016–0

Printed and bound in the EU

Library of Congress Cataloging-in-Publication Data
is available on file.

Contents

Note

The present text derives from one of a number of manuscripts that have been in the possession of my family for some years. I cannot be certain of their origin, but my maternal grandfather was both a medical man and a contemporary of Watson in the RAMC during the Great War. It is the eighth of the documents I have edited for publication, the others being *Sherlock Holmes and the Railway Maniac* (Constable, 1994; A & B Books, 2000), *Sherlock Holmes and the Devil's Grail* (Constable, 1995; A & B Books, 2000), *Sherlock Holmes and the Man from Hell* (Constable, 1997; Linford Mystery Library, 2000), *Sherlock Holmes and the Royal Flush* (Constable, 1998), *The Mystery of the Addleton Curse* (in *The Mammoth Book of New Sherlock Holmes Adventures*, Carroll & Graf Publishers, 1998), *Sherlock Holmes and the Harvest of Death* (Constable, 1999) and 'The Disappearance of Daniel Question' (*Strand Magazine*, USA, April 2000).

As always, I have sought evidence to establish that this is indeed one of the previously unpublished records of a Sherlock Holmes case, but the proof is difficult, the more so since no unassailable sample of Watson's handwriting is known to exist. The fruits of my researches will be found in the notes at the end of the text and, with such assistance as those give, readers must make up their own minds as to the authenticity of the text. Personally, I am as satisfied as reason permits.

Barrie Roberts

Chapter One

A Very Peculiar Parcel

Readers of my earlier accounts of the cases of my friend Mr Sherlock Holmes will recall that it was in April of 1894 that he made his sudden and dramatic reappearance in London after an absence of three years.* During his absence I had lost my beloved wife so that with his return it was an easy matter for me to rid myself of a medical practice, which had become a burden without my dear helpmate, and to move back into our old diggings at 221b Baker Street. Holmes only ever made one reference to my loss, but his unspoken sympathy was a continuing comfort to me at that time and to be once again associated with him in his remarkable enquiries did much to distract me from my grief.

It was in early May of that year, when I had only just resumed my place at Baker Street, that the appalling and astonishing affair of Crosby the banker came into my friend's hands. Holmes had come to breakfast late, as he often did, and sat, still in his dressing-gown, examining the morning papers. He flung the last one to the floor,

* See *The Final Problem* and *The Empty House* by Sir Arthur Conan Doyle.

poured himself another cup of tea and leaned back in his chair, stretching his long arms wide.

'There is nothing – nothing, Watson – in today's prints that promises the least interest,' he said. 'Sometimes I wonder that I troubled to return. There were subjects of investigation far more worthy of my skills in Tibet alone. Have I told you that the Head Lama entreated me to stay and apply my talents to the tracking of the yeti, a mysterious and seemingly half-human beast that haunts the inhospitable upper regions of the Himalayas?'

His comments filled me with alarm. I recognised this mood of dissatisfaction and I was not then aware that somewhere in the course of his three years abroad he had succeeded in freeing himself from the toils of cocaine. 'Something is bound to turn up,' I ventured. 'There is a headless and disfigured cadaver taken from the Thames yesterday,' I suggested by way of encouragement.

'Something will turn up!' he snapped. 'Really, Watson, you demean yourself! As to headless corpses in the Thames – the River Police are forever retrieving the remains of those who drank too well and fell in or those whose end was assisted by a knife or blackjack in some Deptford tavern brawl. I doubt that some pitiful remains mangled by the propellers of the river's traffic will offer us any interest.'

He stood up abruptly and strode to the window, jerking back the curtain and gazing disconsolately into the street. Suddenly the tone of his voice altered.

'Hullo!' he exclaimed, 'here is Lestrade coming with a box under his arm. We may find some stimulus yet. Watson, be so good as to ring for Mrs Hudson to clear away our breakfast and bring a fresh pot of tea.'

Minutes later the little rat-featured Inspector was seated in the basket chair, his hands clasping what seemed to be an ordinary shoebox tied with string.

'So,' began my friend, 'what brings you here this

morning, Lestrade? I had thought that being rid of me for three years, the Yard might have learned to go its own way.'

Lestrade smiled. 'Personally, Mr Holmes, I was delighted to learn that you were back in the land of the living, so to speak. If we have not always agreed, you have always been good enough to share your thoughts with us, which is why I thought you might like a look at this parcel.'

He lifted the box onto the table.

Holmes walked around it. 'A perfectly commonplace shoebox, tied about with ordinary office string. What does it contain, Lestrade?'

'It's the contents that I came about,' said the detective, as Holmes opened his pocket knife. 'We received a very peculiar parcel at the Yard yesterday. It's in that box with all its wrapping. I thought you would like to see it as nearly as possible as it reached us.'

Holmes nodded his approval. 'You are learning, Lestrade, you are learning.' He cut the string around the box and sniffed the package before raising the lid. From the interior he lifted an object wrapped in brown paper and placed it on the table, and from a corner of the box he took a length of dark, coarse string. 'The string has been untied, Lestrade,' he said, holding it up. 'Why was that?'

'Why, Mr Holmes, to get at the contents of course.'

'It should have been cut, Lestrade, thereby preserving the knot. Knots are distinctive and informative. The Quipu Indians of South America had knots so complex and subtle that they could record their people's history and theology in lengths of knotted cord. All I can tell you of this is that it is tarred twine of a kind common in the pockets of seamen. The knot might have confirmed the sender's profession. Very few landsmen can tie a decent knot, but when they do it is usually one of a kind distinctive to their calling.'

He laid the string on the table and with a long index finger began to turn the crumpled brown wrappings away from the contents. At last he succeeded in revealing an object that at first I took to be some sort of vegetable.

It was about the size and shape of a large potato and its surface seemed to have a light brownish colour and a leathery texture. I soon saw that it was not a vegetable, for I noticed that a finely stitched seam ran along one surface of the object. From one end protruded a long strand of black hairs, around which a string had been tied. As Holmes gently prodded it with his long fingers I saw that there were tufts of the same hair elsewhere on its surface.

My friend reached into his pocket for his magnifying glass and examined the object closely. At last he said, 'Unless the published description is widely inaccurate, what we have here is the shrunken head of Algernon Crosby, the missing banker.'

'Great heavens, Holmes!' I exclaimed, while Lestrade sat with dropped jaw. 'You cannot mean that it is a real human head!'

He rolled it so that it faced towards us. It was possible to see that he was right. On the side that had been hidden from Lestrade and me were human features, the eyelids and mouth sewn shut with thread, the eyebrows and whiskers grotesquely large because of the diminution of the head.

Lestrade made a muttered excuse, rose quickly and left the room.

I bent closer to examine the revolting item. 'Is it really a shrunken head, Holmes? I have read of such things but I have never been sure that they actually exist.'

'There is no mistake about it,' he replied. 'The technique of flaying a human skull and shrinking the skin is one of extreme skill. While the application of hot stones and sand to the interior will shrink the skin, skilful moulding of the features is necessary to maintain the relationship of the features during the process. It is a skill possessed by a number of primitive tribes, though mainly, I believe, in South America.'

'But Crosby disappeared in London!' I protested.

'Then it will have been in London that he has been reduced to this form,' said Holmes, and I hope I do him no injustice by suggesting that there was a touch of enthusiasm in his voice at the thought of such a bizarre incident occurring within his bailiwick.

Lestrade rejoined us, looking several shades paler and wiping his mouth with a handkerchief. 'I'm sorry, gentlemen,' he said. 'But I was quite overtaken when you explained what that – that thing – is, Mr Holmes. When it came to the Yard we all thought it was some kind of a jest. We thought it was made of leather and that some saddler or tanner we'd upset was having a joke at our expense. Are you sure that it is Mr Crosby?'

'I cannot be entirely certain,' admitted Holmes, 'but this is the head of a man who kept himself well. When he died he was recently, and skilfully, shaved. His hair had been cut with equal skill and dressed with an expensive preparation. You can see the blackness of the hair, eyebrows and whiskers. That is because they are dyed, but it was professionally done. Unless you have lost another middle-aged wealthy man with heavy black eyebrows, thick whiskers and grey hair dyed black, Lestrade, then I believe that this is Crosby.'

'But what on earth can have happened to him?' the detective wondered.

'He has been murdered – in furtherance of vengeance and most probably by a foreigner. Beyond that you must assist me,' said Holmes. 'I know only what I have read in the newspapers – that Algernon Crosby, a director of the Cork Commercial Bank, was missing from home and his usual haunts, and that fears for his safety were being expressed. When I have told you a little more about your parcel you may fill in the details.'

'Why do you say for vengeance, Mr Holmes?' asked Lestrade.

'Because of the treatment of the head. The practice is usually adopted in order to protect the perpetrator from the victim's vengeance and to enslave the victim's soul. That argues a powerfully emotional motive. As to the nationality or race of the perpetrator . . .'

'You don't believe a white man could have done such a thing?' interrupted the little detective.

Holmes laughed aloud. 'My dear Lestrade,' he said, 'if Scotland Yard follows that belief it will not get very far! The white races of our species have proved themselves many times over to be at least the equal of the black, brown, red and yellow races when it comes to barbarism, if not their superior. I was merely about to remark that the practice of shrinking heads is known among the Jivaros of South America and also various tribes in the Orient. I doubt that you will find a white man who has mastered the techniques involved.'

'You said that you can tell me more?' enquired Lestrade.

'There are certain indications,' replied my friend. 'Tell me, was Crosby a yachtsman?'

'Now that was in the newspapers, Mr Holmes,' said Lestrade, in a disappointed tone. 'He owned *Gyrfalcon*, the prizewinner.'

'Really?' said Holmes. 'I have an almost total lack of interest in the pastimes of the wealthy and as to sports, I always consult Watson. I dare say he has wagered a guinea or two on Crosby at one time or another. I merely commented on the point because this wrapping paper came from a chandler's store – one that provides for yachtsmen.'

'How can you tell?' I asked.

He moved the paper on the table so that the sunlight

from the window fell across it. 'Observe', he commanded, 'that deep crease across the middle. You may be
able to distinguish a faint deposit of some crystalline
substance that has adhered to the fold.'

'But what is it?' I demanded.

'You recall that I sniffed the box before ever undoing
it? That was because I had detected a mixture of odours
arising from it. One I have now determined to be the
bay rum preparation with which Crosby's hair was
dressed. The other is a coarser scent. Take a sniff,
Watson.'

I bent over the paper and did indeed detect a faint
trace of something reminiscent of antiseptics mingled
with a sweeter, sicklier smell. 'There is an antiseptic
there, mixed with something else. Perhaps something to
mask the sharpness of the antiseptic.'

'Well done, Watson! You have been on private
yachts?'

'I have.'

'Then you will have come across that peculiar combi-
nation before. I believe that the deposit on the paper is
of a substance known as Perfumed Anti-Zymotic Crystals. They are used to dispel the grosser odours from the
living quarters of private yachts. More robust seamen do
not put themselves to the expense.'

'Then he was killed on his yacht!' exclaimed Lestrade.

'I did not say so', said Holmes. 'Surely you will have
examined the missing man's yacht?'

'We cannot find it – her, Mr Holmes,' admitted Lestrade. 'Normally he kept *Gyrfalcon* on the Itchen and had
any work done by Morris's yard at Eacham, but Morris
says he hasn't seen *Gyrfalcon* for weeks. He was surprised, because the regatta season is just beginning and
he expected Mr Crosby to put her in for an overhaul
before he started racing her.'

'And she has not gone abroad?'

'Not so far as we can tell, Mr Holmes. The big yachts like *Gyrfalcon* are pretty well-known on the Continent as well as in England.'

'She may, of course, have been disguised,' said Holmes.

'We have circulated her particulars, Mr Holmes. I don't know what more we can do,' said Lestrade.

'You might,' Holmes suggested, 'enquire of the London Patent Automatic Disinfection Company as to their customers in London.'

'The London Patent . . .' began the detective before he grasped my friend's remark. 'Ah! The manufacturers of the – of the crystals.'

'Precisely!' Holmes nodded.

'But why do you believe that the crime was committed in London, Mr Holmes?'

'Because the postmark on the wrapping of your parcel reveals that it was sent from Charing Cross. The idea of a sender who wished not to be identified carrying a parcel containing a shrunken head very far is one that does not occur to me as very likely.'

Lestrade nodded.

'I suggest, also, that the sender is not British. He spells "Scotland" with a double "t" – not, I would think, an error that even a semi-literate Briton would make. Nor is he familiar with London, insofar as he seems not to be aware that your headquarters stand on the Embankment.'

'This has been very useful, Mr Holmes, and I am grateful,' said the Inspector. 'Now I'd best be away and see to that enquiry about the crystals.'

'You will do no such thing, Lestrade,' stated Holmes. 'You will take a cheroot from the coal scuttle and tell us all that you know of the late Algernon Crosby.'

Chapter Two

The Late Algernon Crosby

As the little detective found himself a cheroot, cut and lit it, Holmes and I filled our pipes in preparation for his narrative. Holmes, I was pleased to observe, with his pipe well alight, began rubbing one palm with the thumb of the opposing hand, a sure sign that he expected cerebral stimulation.

Once his cheroot was well aglow, Lestrade pulled out a notebook and thumbed through its pages. 'Algernon Desmond Crosby', he began, 'is – was – forty-one years old. He was the eldest son of Colonel Crosby, whose family have owned extensive estates in Ireland for generations. Our Crosby – Algernon, that is – was educated at Cork Academy and Cambridge. He married in 1875 and established his married home at Bradon Lodge in Hampshire. He was a sportsman at school and at Cambridge, and a member of the Cork Yacht Club. Once settled in England he became a member of the best yachting clubs. He had a decent income from his interest in the Cork Commercial Bank – he inherited the majority interest on his father's death – and, when not abroad, followed the regattas, frequently winning major contests. For example, in 1892 he won the Enticott Cup at Cowes with a boat called *Esmerelde*.'

'He must', Holmes interrupted, 'have enjoyed more than a decent income in order to follow the regattas and compete throughout the season. Have you any idea what it costs to maintain a sporting vessel and crew? What was *Esmerelde*'s tonnage?'

Lestrade flicked the pages of his notebook. 'I don't have it, Mr Holmes, but his last boat, *Gyrfalcon*, was thirty-five tons.'

'Did he buy her or have her built?' Holmes asked.

'She was built for him, Mr Holmes. By Aldhous and Rushbrook at Brightlingsea.'

'She will have cost him about a thousand to build. To maintain such a vessel in the regattas can cost about four hundred a season. He was a wealthy man.'

I silently noted Holmes's ready calculation of the figures, despite his earlier claim to have no knowledge of rich men's sports, but it was characteristic of him that he understated the extent of his encyclopaedic memory.

Lestrade merely whistled softly at the size of the figures.

'You may say so, Mr Holmes! Apart from his income from the Bank, there were his estates in Ireland, though he has sold off a lot of the land since his father's death.'

'Why was that?' demanded Holmes.

'Why, I believe that he was just establishing himself in England, rather than in Ireland. Once his mother was gone he even sold off the old house in Ireland, though that had been in the family for donkeys' years.'

'Who benefits by his death? Is his wife still living?' asked Holmes.

'Yes, Mr Holmes. He had a wife and two young sons, fourteen and twelve. His eldest son will inherit on coming of age.'

'Meanwhile,' said Holmes, 'the inheritance may well be controlled by the widow. Carry on, Lestrade. How did his disappearance arise?'

'We don't know exactly how or when he vanished, Mr Holmes. He left his home in Hampshire on a Thursday, six weeks ago, saying that he was going up to town and that he expected to return by the Sunday. He didn't come back and, on Monday, Mrs Crosby telephoned his club, which was where he usually stayed while in London. It seems he had dined at the club on Sunday evening with two friends and signed the bill, but he had not been staying there.'

'You have spoken to his dining companions?' asked Holmes.

'Oh, yes, Mr Holmes. All they can say is that he claimed to have come up to London on a piece of business – which he did not specify – and seemed quite normal.'

'Why were Scotland Yard so sure that he had not taken his yacht out if she is missing?' asked Holmes.

'Because we know when she left her mooring. She was taken out of the Itchen on Saturday night. The watchman at Morris's yard saw her go out.'

'And who was on board her? Was Crosby himself on her?'

'Hampshire Police say that the watchman saw one person go aboard her and he thinks that was a man whom he called "Teddy the American".'

'Who', demanded Holmes, 'is "Teddy the American"?'

'Apparently he's a yacht hand whom Crosby hired in the West Indies last year. After the regatta season Crosby took *Gyrfalcon* abroad. He crossed the Atlantic and visited some of the yachting centres in America, then dropped down to the West Indies. When he returned he had this American on board and he kept him on a retainer in England.'

'Presumably', said Holmes, 'Crosby took a crew across the Atlantic and brought one back with him. Were they the same men – apart from the American?'

'Yes, sir,' Lestrade confirmed. 'He took three men and a boy out with him, and brought the same four back, and also the American.'

'That', remarked Holmes, 'may be significant. If he needed four men, he would surely have taken four on a voyage across the Atlantic. After all, he must have known *Gyrfalcon* well, and been familiar with her behaviour and requirements, but he brought back an extra man. Was he a seaman, I wonder?'

'It appears so, Mr Holmes. We have spoken to all of the crew and they say as the American seemed to know yachts well.'

'What has happened to *Gyrfalcon*'s crew? Have they disappeared with her?'

'No, Mr Holmes. When they came back to England they were all paid off, apart from the captain, Captain Napley. Napley was kept on his usual retainer out of season and Crosby told him that he should want him again once the season began, but he never heard from him.'

'You say that the yard at Eacham was expecting to have the boat in?'

'Yes, Mr Holmes. Morris says that when the yacht came in from the West Indies he was told by Crosby that he would be taking her out again for one short trip and that after that Morris could have her to put in order in time for Harwich Regatta.'

'But Crosby never returned. Instead, the American took *Gyrfalcon* out to some unknown destination and Crosby is dead,' mused Holmes.

'Evidently Crosby was not intending suicide,' I remarked, and immediately wished that I had remained silent.

'Watson,' said Holmes, 'sometimes I despair of you!

Even if Crosby committed suicide – which I very much doubt – he certainly did not reduce himself to that state!' And he pointed to the object on the table.

'No,' he continued, 'Crosby was killed as an act of vengeance.'

'But what for, Mr Holmes?' asked Lestrade.

'That', said Holmes, 'is one of the two questions about which the whole matter turns – for what and by whom?' And he knocked out his pipe on the grate.

Lestrade took himself off and as his footfalls faded down the stairs Holmes smiled to himself. 'There is', he remarked, 'an obvious aspect of the matter, which seems to have completely escaped Lestrade's notice.'

'What's that?' I enquired.

'Why, if I am right in believing that his parcel contained the head of Crosby the banker, then there must be at least one more portion of him somewhere.'

Chapter Three

The Chandler's Shop

By next morning Lestrade had remedied his oversight. He called upon us early, bringing with him a list of chandlers who supplied Perfumed Anti-Zymotic Crystals and the news that there was a headless cadaver in the River Police's mortuary.

Holmes glanced briefly at Lestrade's list, then slid it into his coat pocket. 'Be so good as to ring for our boots, Watson,' he requested, 'we have a visit to make.'

In a very short time we were at the mortuary, where my friend asked me my opinion of the corpse that was displayed to us.

I had seen plenty of mutilations on the battlefield and in the hospital, and had steeled myself for the decapitated body lying under the sheet, but I admit that I was unprepared for the other evidence, which was revealed when the mortuary attendant pulled back the sheet. 'Great heavens, Holmes!' I exclaimed. 'This poor wretch has been tortured!'

'So it would appear,' my friend agreed, 'but I would still value your observations, Watson.'

I took a deep breath and began my examination. 'It is

a man of about forty,' I said. 'In good health and good condition for his age. He had very little surplus flesh and his muscles appear well-developed. Although his fingernails are well-manicured, his hands are not those of an entirely sedentary individual. There are slight calluses on them.'

I examined the hideous wound that showed where the head had been removed.

'The head was not removed by accident in the river,' I continued. 'It was cut from the body with a single skilled blow of a heavy but sharp implement, probably an axe. The chafed areas at the wrists and ankles show that he was tightly bound for some time.'

'You believe that the small marks all over the torso are indications of torture?' enquired Holmes.

'Indubitably,' I stated. 'Those are the marks of repeated applications of a lighted cigarette or some such. The smaller marks are wounds from the point of an extremely sharp knife, which has cut without penetrating very far. It is quite horrible, Holmes. A number of these wounds have partly healed. It was not done all at once. Some scoundrel has repeatedly applied a knife-point and a lighted cigarette to this poor wretch's body over a period of days.'

Holmes leaned forward and examined several of the wounds with his lens. 'You are right,' he said, straightening up, 'some of them are partly healed, though I think the burns are from a cheroot, not a cigarette.'

'I don't suppose it will have mattered very much to the victim,' I muttered.

'Perhaps not,' said Holmes, 'but it matters to me. It is highly improbable that a regular smoker of either cigarettes or cheroots would change his habits solely to facilitate torture. He will have used the implement most readily at hand, whereby we have learned that he is a smoker of cheroots. I take it that we can be reasonably certain that this is Crosby?' he asked Lestrade.

'Oh, indeed, Mr Holmes. You can see where we removed a signet ring from his hand. That is being taken to Hampshire at present for Mrs Crosby to identify, so as to spare her being brought here.'

Holmes nodded. 'Well then, Lestrade, if that is Crosby, then you are looking for a man of some considerable strength, who smokes cheroots, is left-handed and is almost certainly not a white man.'

'Left-handed?' queried the detective.

'Yes,' Holmes answered. 'If Watson is right about the removal of the head with an axe – and I am sure that he is – then our man is left-handed.'

'I don't think I follow you, Holmes,' I said. 'We do not know at what angle the killer stood when he struck the blow.'

'It is immaterial,' replied Holmes. 'Since it is impossible to hold an axe equally with both hands, there is always a twist applied by the arms as the implement swings. The direction of that twist is determined by the right- or left-handedness of the person swinging the axe and is reflected in the cut made by the blade. It is clear from the cut that Crosby was struck from somewhere behind him and equally clear that his killer is left-handed.'

'As well as being connected with yachting,' observed Lestrade.

'No,' said Holmes sharply. 'I have not said as much because the connection cannot, at present, be confirmed. All we know is that his wrapping paper came from a yacht chandler. Come, Watson – we have enquiries to make. Good day, Lestrade.'

Some of the addresses on Lestrade's list were close to the mortuary, so that we made our way on foot, along streets that seemed to consist entirely of public houses, cheap eating places and shops selling seamen's clothing, ships' supplies, marine hardware or all three. The air reeked of tar and timber, rope and spices. Among the passers-by on the pavements were people of many races, Chinese, Arabs, Lascars, Africans, Indians – if there was an area of London in which we might find such a man as Holmes had described, we seemed to be in the heart of it.

Three of the shops listed we visited without success, their owners pointing out that, while they sold the crystals, they did no large business in them, usually bought them in against a specific order and had not done so recently All the shopkeepers pointed out to us that few yachtsmen or their skippers ever brought their vessels this far up the Thames.

The fourth shop we entered was like all the others – suits of sea clothing, oilskins and boots hung in clusters outside; inside was a large, gloomy cavern crammed with clothing, tools, rope, paint and a thousand sea-going necessaries, the place reeking with a mixture of linseed and paraffin, rope and tar, paint and leather, candles and varnish.

Graby, its owner, was an unprepossessing individual who chewed tobacco continuously, spat regularly and had the habit of never looking his interlocutor in the eye. Nevertheless he admitted readily enough that he had Perfumed Anti-Zymotic Crystals in stock. 'They was an order', he explained, 'for a gent as called here sometimes.'

'And what might be that gentleman's name?' asked Holmes as a coin flashed briefly between his fingers.

'I could look it up,' said Graby, letting his wandering eyes rest briefly on the coin while he groped beneath his counter for a ledger. Pulling it out, he thumbed through its pages for a while. 'Here it is!' he said at last and read the entry. '"Anti-Zymotic Crystals for Mr Crosby." That's the last time as I had them.' And his hand moved as fast as a conjurer's to take my friend's coin.

'And did he collect them?' asked Holmes, his own hand withdrawing the coin to a safe distance.

'No, he didn't collect them. He told me when they was in to give them to his skipper.'

'Captain Napley?' queried Holmes.

'Napley? No, he's not called Napley. He's an American called Danziger – Teddy Danziger.'

'Are you sure?' asked Holmes.

'Sure? Of course I'm sure! He lived here, didn't he?'

'Who lived here?' I interjected.

'Why, Teddy Danziger – Crosby's skipper.'

I looked at Holmes in bewilderment, knowing that the captain of *Gyrfalcon* was called Napley, but my friend appeared completely unsurprised.

'What manner of man is Captain Danziger?' Holmes enquired. 'What does he look like?'

'He's a big bloke, light-brown hair, greyish eyes, weathered skin. Looks about thirty-five, might be older.'

'Anything else about him?' pressed my friend.

Graby's fingers picked at a patch on his counter where a pool of linseed oil had spilled and hardened. 'I seen him once with his shirt off and he had scars,' he said.

'What sort of scars?' Holmes asked.

'Peculiar, they was. All over his back. Like patterns had been drawn on him with a sharp knife.'

'Does Captain Danziger still live here?' Holmes wanted to know.

Graby shook his head. 'No,' he said. 'Crosby came to see him one Saturday morning and Danziger went off with him. Said he'd be away a couple of days, but he ain't come back.'

Holmes added another coin to the one in his hand and laid them both on the counter. 'Has Danziger's room been let again?' he asked. 'Might we see it?'

The coins had been swallowed up by Graby's dirty hand but he did not look co-operative. 'Look here,' he said, 'I've answered your questions polite enough, when some wouldn't have done, but I ain't at all sure I ought to let you look in my lodger's room.'

'It may help you to decide', said Holmes quietly but firmly, 'if I explain to you that my colleague and I are associated with Inspector Lestrade of Scotland Yard in investigating the murder of your lodger's employer, Mr Crosby.'

Graby's dirty face paled. 'Well then, you should have said,' he mumbled. 'It's just that there's been others.'

'Others?' asked Holmes. 'Seeking to see Danziger's room? Did you permit it?'

'Of course not,' said the chandler. 'He wasn't official. I don't know what kind of cove he was.'

'So there has been one person enquiring after Danziger,' mused my friend. 'When was that?'

'It was the very evening he went away and that's another reason why I never let him. I thought as Teddy was coming back then and what would he have said if he knew I'd been letting all and sundry into his private premises?'

'Very proper, I'm sure,' said Holmes. 'What was this unprepossessing caller like?'

'He was a foreigner – a darkie. I supposed he was some kind of seaman.'

'How did you know he was a foreigner?'

'By his looks and the way he spoke. He hadn't much English and he was brown-skinned – you know, with long black hair. I thought he was an Indian or a Malay or something like that.'

'And all he wanted was to see Danziger's room?'

'Yes, but I told him. my lodger's room was private. I mean, it had been paid for then. Not like now when I ain't seen hide nor hair of Teddy for weeks, nor heard a word from him.'

'But you have no objection to our examining the room, Mr Graby?'

'Well, you're different, aren't you? You're the official police'.

'We are not', said Holmes, 'the official police. I am a consulting detective who is assisting Scotland Yard.' And he followed Graby through the rear door of the shop.

.

Chapter Four

Danziger's Room

Graby led us through a dark rear hallway to the foot of a steep flight of stairs, where he pressed a key into Holmes's hand. 'All the way to the top,' he said, pointing. 'It's on the left at the top, the attic. I'd come up with you, but got to mind the shop.'

He turned away and we climbed steadily up two flights of stairs to reach a small landing with only one door opening from it.

As Holmes unlocked the door he stretched out a hand to prevent me entering. He stood for a moment in the open doorway, surveying the room and sniffing the air, scenting like some tall beast of prey. After a moment he turned. 'You may enter, Watson'.

I followed him into a large, L-shaped room. It had a ceiling that slanted towards the outer wall in which a single small sash window let in a little light through its unwashed panes. I crossed the room and looked out of the window, seeing that it looked down upon a narrow unpaved alley behind the row of shops.

Holmes, meanwhile, was taking stock of the room's contents, which were few. A small brass bedstead with a jumble of bedclothes heaped upon it lay in the smaller portion of the L and beside it a red-painted wicker table with a top of cracked tiles. A Barclay and Perkins Brewery ashtray lay on the table, well filled with cigar stubs.

Holmes riffled his fingertips through the stubs, picked up one and sniffed it briefly. 'Cheap West Indian,' he commented, dropping the butt back into the ashtray.

A small deal table with a grimy top stood beneath the window. Holmes examined its surface carefullly with his lens, then turned his attention to the window frame.

I had looked beneath the bed, discovering a pair of battered boots and a canvas kitbag of the type that seamen carry, together with a cracked but gaudy china chamberpot whose odour underlined Danziger's long absence from his lodgings. I dragged out the boots and bag, and examined them. The boots surprised me. So far from being seaboots, they were American riding boots of the Western pattern, with high heels, now badly worn, and elaborate decoration, which suggested that they had once been costly. Laying them aside, I turned to the bag.

Its weight surprised me when I lifted it to the tabletop. Inside I found at first nothing but a few items of clothing, guernseys, shirts and stockings, but at the bottom my fingers touched something cold and hard, and I drew out a large pistol.

Holmes had finished his exploration of the window frame and joined me. 'Look here.' I said to him, indicating the boots and the pistol. 'The man seems to have been as much of a cowboy as a seaman.'

Holmes picked up the boots and pointed to marks of wear across the insteps and slight abrasions about the ankles. 'These boots have been worn for some long time with spurs,' he remarked. 'There are the marks of the strap that holds the spur in place and here are the small incisions caused when the spur on one boot catches against the other boot.'

I held up the gun. 'Well,' I said, 'he may have been a horseman, but he was no gunman. This is an old Colt cap-and-ball pistol.'

Holmes took the gun from me, broke the breech and peered through the barrel. 'It is certainly an old weapon,' he confirmed, 'and not used recently, but it is the weapon of an experienced gunfighter.'

'Really?' I said. 'Surely it would be too slow?'

He shook his head. 'Bat Masterson, who knew more than a little about small arms, once told me that the best pistol shot he knew always used a cap-and-ball weapon, as did many of that breed. They believed that cartridge ammunition caused the weapon to jerk more vigorously when it exploded, thereby spoiling the aim. Besides,' he added, 'observe this, Watson.' He held out the weapon and pulled the trigger rapidly. I was surprised at how fast the pistol's mechanism responded. 'That's fast for an old pistol,' I said.

'Precisely,' he agreed. 'This weapon has been adapted for the most rapid fire. The trigger mechanism has been filed to make it slip more quickly, reducing the time taken for the hammer to rise and fall between shots. In addition the owner of this weapon has been accustomed to "fanning" it.' He showed me where the dark blue-black finish of the weapon was missing from the top of the hammer.

'Why would that be?' I asked.

'As the right hand operates the trigger, the edge of the left palm is struck against the top of the hammer so as to pull it back fast. The altered trigger mechanism then allows it to fall faster, both effects considerably reducing the delay between shots. An old weapon this certainly is, Watson, but it is definitely the weapon of a skilled gunfighter.'

I delved again into the seabag, finding only a few pieces of paper left. The larger of them turned out to be a handsomely engraved document, its decorative border displaying mermen with tridents and a nautical crown. The text read:

> At the Court of His Marine Majesty King Neptune, Ruler of all Seas and Oceans, Lakes, Rivers, Ponds, Streams and Puddles. Know all men by these presents that .... has on ....
> Crossed the Line and is by that act admitted into our Ancient Company of Mermen and Mermaids whereby he is now a Freeman of all Waters under our Command wheresoever in the world.

The blank spaces had been filled with the name 'Edmund Danziger' and a date some years gone.

I was familiar with sailors' Crossing the Line certificates and laid it aside, but the next item, a smaller document, astonished me. A slip of yellow paper the size of a handbill, it announced in ornate lettering:

YE OLDE WHOREHOUSE
Sacramento Street,
San Francisco.
COOL DRINKS + LOVELY GIRLS + GOOD FOOD
+ MUSIC

Holmes saw the expression on my face and smiled. 'I can assure you that there is', he told me, 'such an establishment in San Francisco.'

'I do not doubt it,' I said. 'It was merely the vulgarity of its name and the openness of its advertising that brought me up short.'

The third paper was another of the same kind, but gave me an even greater surprise, for it stated:

THE FINEST GIRLS IN TOWN
Madame Lu-Ann's
Holmes Street, Tiger Bay

'Surely,' I cried, 'they do not permit this kind of thing in Cardiff, of all places?'

Holmes laughed outright. 'I'm sure that the activity goes on in that city. It would be a rare seaport where it did not. However, I think you will find that Holmes Street is in Tiger Bay, Demerara, not Cardiff, though I cannot vouch for the services of Madame Lu-Ann.'

He took the papers from my hand and examined them more carefully than I thought they warranted, then lifted them to his nostrils. 'I thought as much!' he exclaimed. 'Our friend Mr Graby has been looking into his lodger's affairs, for all his pretence of confidentiality.'

'How can you tell?' I asked.

'Did you not note', he said, 'how his fingers teased that puddle of dried linseed on his counter top? These papers are spattered with grubby fingermarks, which might, indeed, have come from any one of a thousand sources, but happen to smell strongly of linseed oil. I think it a reasonable inference that one of the burglars of this room was Graby.'

'One of them!' I exclaimed.

'Certainly,' he said and stepped towards the window, beckoning me to follow. 'You see', he continued, 'that the only catch on this window is the ordinary swivel device, set on the top of the lower sash frame.'

I nodded.

He thrust the lower frame upwards and bent to look underneath it. I followed suit. 'Observe,' he said. 'A fine sliver of wood has been removed from the inner edge of the upper frame. That is where a knife blade has been slipped between the frames in order to force the catch over to the open position.'

I looked from the open window into the alley below. 'It's a deuced long way,' I said, 'and there's only the drainpipe. Whoever forced that window was by way of being a fearless and skilful climber.'

'True, Watson,' he agreed, 'but that is not the only curious feature of the matter.'

He pointed to the lower edge of the window frame, drawing my attention to a faint mark upon it. It seemed as though something dusty and shapeless had rested there, and there were tiny streaks of green around it. 'What do you make of that?' Holmes demanded.

'It is surely the mark of a knee, where the burglar has knelt on the frame before entering or before leaving,' I suggested.

My friend shook his head. 'No, no! That will not suffice. What of the green marks?'

'Perhaps he had grass stains about his trousers,' I hazarded.

'Watson, you are inventing theories to fit the facts,' he chided, 'not permitting the facts to lead you to an explanatory theory. A knee would have left a rounder imprint than that, even a fat knee, and it was not a fat man who climbed that pipe. Here – look at this!' He pointed to the top of the deal table below the window. 'What is that?' he asked.

He was indicating a place on the table where a spilled liquid had dried thinly on the wooden surface. Upon that area could be a seen a faint pattern, as though a coarse cloth had been pressed against the stain. The patterned area seemed to be an oval of about a foot in length, though one end was missing, having extended beyond the stain.

'An elbow or a sleeve laid carelessly on the table?' I suggested.

Holmes snorted. 'Even the most robust of elbows leaves only a small impression and the mark of a sleeved arm is likely to be more or less rectangular. That is the mark of a foot.'

'A foot!' I exclaimed.

'From the window, Watson, you may observe that the unpaved alley has large clumps of grass growing at its sides. Whoever climbed that drainpipe and forced the window wrapped his feet in cloths stuffed with grass.'

'I have seen country people do that,' I remarked, 'when they have an injury to a foot or when their boots are badly broken.'

Holmes stared at me. 'If I did not know you well, Watson,' he said, 'I should despair of you! Our burglar was not a crippled yokel, nor were his boots out of repair. He muffled his feet for silence and so as to leave no footprint.'

He swivelled, casting a keen glance about the shabby room. 'Come, Watson,' he said, 'we have learned all that we can here.'

Chapter Five

Crosby's Bequest

'Now, Watson,' said Holmes, 'let us consider what we have learned.'

We had gone from Graby's chandlery to a nearby public house and were seated in a corner with our ale. The tavern was typical of the area, filled with all manner of seamen from every part of the world. I was always a little nervous of such places, being uncomfortably aware of the speed with which violence could erupt in them and of the foreign habit of carrying concealed knives, but Holmes seemed completely at ease in them. I sometimes wonder if his frequent ventures into the East End and the docks in disguise were not, in part, an excuse to mingle more freely in their polyglot society or to release, in whatever guise he wore, aspects of himself that were otherwise unsatisfied. I was musing along these lines when his remark recalled me to our business.

'We have established that Crosby did employ an American seaman called Teddy Danziger,' I commented.

'Indeed,' said my friend, 'and we have some confirmation of Lestrade's information that Crosby brought

Danziger back from the West Indies, inasmuch as Danziger was evidently familiar with the seats of pleasure in Demerara and smoked West Indian cigars.'

The mention of cigars brought back an unpleasant recollection. 'Do you believe that Danziger is the man who tortured poor Crosby?' I asked.

Holmes shook his head impatiently. 'Did I not point out to you that Crosby's burns were inflicted with a cheroot? Danziger's cigar ends were too big. Besides, if Graby and the watchman at Eacham can be believed, Danziger was somewhere at sea when Crosby disappeared.'

'Where do you think he went?' I enquired. 'Might he have returned to America?'

'He might,' Holmes answered, 'but it is highly improbable, not least because he would have required some minimal crew to work *Gyrfalcon* across the Atlantic. He told Graby that he would be away for a few days and he left behind him his seabag and his pistol. He was not expecting a long absence and he was not expecting any trouble. Nevertheless, I would like a word with Mr Danziger.'

'Why do you think Graby called him Crosby's captain?' I asked.

'It is certainly curious,' he said. 'Lestrade told us that Crosby had kept Captain Napley on his usual retainer, yet Graby was clearly under the impression that Danziger was Crosby's captain and he can only have received that impression from the American or Crosby or both. That is, I think, a point on which Graby was telling us all the truth he knew.'

'You believe that he was less than frank with us?' I wondered.

'Do you not?' he responded 'Occasion may arise to revisit Mr Graby and ask him why he searched his lodger's room and whether he removed anything.'

'You believe that something was missing?'

'We know that two people burgled Danziger's room – one at no little risk. That suggests that there may have been something unusual to attract them more than a working seaman's odds and ends. One of them – and it may easily have been Graby – might have got his hands on whatever it was.'

'Have you any idea what it may have been that attracted them?'

'If I knew that, Watson, I should be a great deal closer to the solution of this problem. What I do know is that we must pay a visit to Hampshire tomorrow.'

Bradon Lodge stood alone between two nondescript hamlets in the hinterland of Southampton. On approaching it I noted that it was a large, modern building, more discreetly reminiscent of an old-fashioned manor house than many of its age. Wide lawns and handsome trees flanked the carriageway, and colourful flowerbeds lay beneath the ground-floor windows.

An elderly manservant, entirely in black, answered our ring at the door. 'I very much regret, gentlemen, that Mrs Crosby is in mourning and is not receiving visitors,' he informed us.

'Please give your mistress our deepest sympathies,' said Holmes, 'and show her this. I think that you will find that she would wish to see us.' He pressed his card into the old man's hand.

'Very well, sir,' said that official. 'I will inform Mrs Crosby that Mr Sherlock Holmes wishes to speak to her. Perhaps you would wait in the hall.'

He admitted us to the hallway and left us there. Soon he returned and invited us to follow him, leading us to a rear sitting room where Mrs Crosby, clad in the heavy mourning that was fashionable before the war made death a frequent visitor, greeted us. She was a woman in her middle thirties, handsomely built, with striking black eyes and strong features.

'Mr Holmes,' she said, 'I am so sorry that Walters tried to send you away, but you will understand my situation.'

'I understand and I sympathise, Mrs Crosby,' said my friend. 'Ordinarily I would not impose upon your grief, but Scotland Yard has seen fit to consult me in the matter of your late husband's death and there may be points on which only you can inform me.'

'I will do anything that I can to assist you, Mr Holmes,' she replied. 'My husband was sometimes rash and foolhardy but he was devoted to me and the children, and I loved him very much. I shall never forget the manner of his death, nor shall I rest until the perpetrator is brought to justice. I implored the County Police to ask for your assistance when first my husband disappeared, but they insisted that they would deal with the matter themselves. I am delighted that Scotland Yard is not making the same mistake, Mr Holmes. If you will both be seated I shall send for some tea and attempt to answer any question that you wish to put.'

'I'm extremely grateful to you,' said Holmes, once we were seated, 'and I apologise in advance if anything which I ask should strike you as impertinent, but at this stage of an investigation any fact, however slight or seemingly irrelevant, may have great importance.'

'I understand that, Mr Holmes. Pray ask your questions.'

'You referred to your late husband as "foolhardy", Mrs Crosby. May I ask why and in what respect?'

'One might imagine', she replied, 'that with Algernon's banking connection he would have been a man who knew how to handle money, Mr Holmes, but that was not the case. I do not know if you are aware that he had to sell off most of his family's holdings in Ireland?'

Holmes nodded and she continued: 'My late husband was a man of great charm, Mr Holmes, and I loved him deeply, but I am forced to admit that, in many ways, Algernon was still a boy. He found the affairs of the Bank and his estates dull, and was never so happy as when he was at sea. I used to say that *Gyrfalcon* was my rival for his affections.'

'And how are your finances at present?' asked Holmes.

'Rather better than might have been expected,' she answered. 'I confess, Mr Holmes, that there have been times when my husband's death would have left the children and me in desperate straits, but I am assured by the Bank that a large sum was recently placed on deposit by Algernon – sufficiently large to ensure that we shall never want.'

'I am pleased to hear it,' said my friend. 'Your late husband seems to have had a pronounced sporting instinct. Was he also a speculator where finance was concerned?'

She smiled reminiscently. 'It was certainly the case that he always believed in the pot of gold at the end of the rainbow, Mr Holmes. Quite a lot of his funds disappeared, I believe, in speculations advised by his friends that came to nothing. For some time he had an interest in treasure-hunting. I recall that, a few years ago, he invested one hundred pounds in a voyage to some Atlantic island where there was supposed to be a fabulous treasure. I felt obliged to point out to him that one does not make a fortune for an investment of one hundred pounds, but all he said was, "Some people discover treasures, my dear. Why shouldn't it be me?" I admit that I was not unhappy that he fell ill shortly before the expedition was due to sail, and so had to forgo the six months of fruitless labour that was the only result.'

'Are you aware', asked Holmes, 'of the source of the

funds which the Bank now holds for you, Mrs Crosby?'

'I am sorry to say that I was so relieved to know that poor Algernon had succeeded in making ample provision for us that I did not question the origins of the funds, Mr Holmes. Should I have done so?'

He shook his head. 'No, Mrs Crosby,' he replied. 'I was merely curious as to the source, but it is not of great significance. Can you tell me anything about a man called Edmund Danziger?'

'Certainly,' she said. 'Danziger is a man whom my husband met in the West Indies on the last occasion he took his yacht across the Atlantic. Algernon engaged him for the return voyage, as he was not entirely satisfied with *Gyrfalcon*'s performance and felt that he might need an extra hand on the return voyage.'

'And do you know where Danziger is now?'

'I do, Mr Holmes. I understand that he decided not to return home and has taken up residence in London. I have an address for him if it will assist you.'

'That would be very useful, Mrs Crosby.'

She touched a bell and when her elderly manservant appeared in response to it instructed him: 'Walters, in the top right-hand pigeon-hole of my husband's writing desk is a white envelope with the name and address of Edmund Danziger written on it. Please bring the envelope to me. The desk is not locked.'

While we awaited Walters's return, the widow turned back to Holmes. 'May I ask what is your interest in Danziger, Mr Holmes? I enquire merely because Scotland Yard appears to believe that he was the man who took *Gyrfalcon* from her mooring in the Itchen.'

'That is partly the reason for my interest in him, Mrs Crosby. Tell me, do you have any inkling of why Danziger took *Gyrfalcon* and where he may have taken her?'

She shook her head. 'No, Mr Holmes. I can only assume that Scotland Yard is right, and that Danziger saw an opportunity to steal my husband's yacht and has taken her abroad.'

Holmes frowned. 'The real opportunity to steal *Gyrfalcon* would not have arisen until after your husband's death, or at least his kidnapping, and we know that Mr Crosby was still alive and free when *Gyrfalcon* left the Itchen. I should tell you', he added, 'that there are indications that the American took *Gyrfalcon* out on your husband's instructions. Furthermore, I am not yet convinced that *Gyrfalcon* has gone abroad. If I may change tack, as it were, can you tell me where I may find Captain Napley?'

'That is easy, Mr Holmes. Until the whereabouts of *Gyrfalcon* are determined and I make up my mind as to her disposal, I have kept Napley on his usual retainer, though I have told him that he may seek casual employment in the regatta season. He should be at his usual lodgings – the Boatman's Arms at Eacham.'

'I wonder if you would allow me to make use of his services, Mrs Crosby?'

'Certainly, Mr Holmes, if it will assist your enquiries.' And she took a black-edged card from her reticule and scribbled a note upon its back. 'That should be sufficient authority for him to help you, Mr Holmes.'

Holmes had taken the card and thanked her when we were interrupted by Walters's return with the envelope. Mrs Crosby took it from him and passed it straight to Holmes. He glanced at the address on the front, then lifted the flap and drew out a single piece of card. Pasted on to it was a sheet of paper bearing a series of words, each followed by a symbol. Holmes scanned the sheet for a moment, then asked, 'Have you any idea what this means, Mrs Crosby?'

'None whatever,' she replied. 'I only know that my husband was most emphatic that, if anything happened to him, this document should go to Danziger.'

Chapter Six

The Second Captain

Eacham was typical of the villages that lie around the mouth of the Itchen, the Beaulieu and the sides of Southampton Water, a crescent of cottages around a green or 'hard', open on one side to the water so that boats built upon it could be slid into the waves. A miscellany of small craft bobbed at the river's edge and larger, sleeker vessels were moored out in the stream.

The Boatman's Arms was a large, sprawling building, part thatched and part tiled, which loomed over a quay at one end of the crescent. Its public bar was filled with weather-beaten faces and noisy with the accents of Southampton Water and other ports, when Holmes and I entered.

A quick word with the landlord as we ordered our drinks told us that Crosby's captain was seated in the corner with two or three friends. The innkeeper pointed out a tall, pipe-smoking man with a close, greying beard and a marine cap.

We took the next table and Holmes caught Napley's eye. 'Captain Napley,' he said, 'I am sorry to interrupt your pleasures, but I wonder if you would be kind enough to join my friend and me to discuss a matter which may be to your advantage.'

Napley made his apologies to his friends, picked up his mug and came across to our table. Holmes waved the sailor to a seat, but he stood, looking both of us over carefully. 'Might I ask', he said, in a ripe Hampshire burr, 'whom I have the honour of addressing?'

'I am Sherlock Holmes and this is my friend Dr Watson,' said Holmes and produced Mrs Crosby's card. 'Your late employer's widow believed that you might be willing to assist me if you could.'

Our guest sat down and read the note on the back of the card. 'Well, of course,' he said, 'it goes without saying as I'd do anything I could to help Mrs Crosby. She's been that good to me. With Mr Crosby dead and *Gyrfalcon* gone she might have put me out of employment, and it's a bad time. With the regatta season starting, everyone's made their arrangements and I should have got nothing unless someone fell ill, and I wouldn't have wished that on nobody.'

Holmes nodded. 'Where do you think *Gyrfalcon* has gone, Captain?'

'There's some say as she's across the Atlantic and others as she's in France. I can't see her going American. She'd need more nor one man to handle her and we'd have heard if Danziger had taken on hands at any port on the south coast.'

'You believe that Danziger took her?'

'Certain sure, Mr Holmes. I've talked to Pally Usher what was watching Morris's yard that night. There's been a bit of thieving, see – timber and paint and that, and Mr Morris he put Pally on to keep an eye on the yard at night. Well, he told me he was sure it was Teddy Danziger as took *Gyrfalcon* out that night. He says he knew him by his build and his walk as he come down the jetty.'

'Danziger limped with the left leg,' said Sherlock Holmes.

'You've met him, then?' asked Napley.

'No, Captain, but I have met his boots and they are the boots of a man who limps on his left leg. What can you tell me of Danziger?'

The sailor chuckled. 'I can tell you why he limps. At least, I know what he told us as we came back from the West Indies. He said as he was once a cowboy in Arizona and that his game leg was the result of not being quite quick enough on the draw. He reckoned as the other fellow got two shots off just as Danziger shot him. One ended up in Ted's leg and the other hit him in the right hand. He said as that made him give up the gun and take to the sea.'

'And did you believe him?' asked Holmes.

'He was a cool customer,' said the Captain. 'We had a few bad little goes coming across but they never bothered him. What's more, he had a gun with him, a pistol, and sometimes, when it was calm, like, he'd practise with it, shooting at seagulls and getting Billy the boy to throw tin cans for him. For all his right hand was crippled, he was quick with that odd gun and he was a good shot with it, so I reckon that's most likely the way he got his limp. He wasn't a bragging sort of fellow.'

Holmes summoned the potboy and had our drinks replenished. 'Why', he enquired, when the potboy had gone about his business, 'did Mr Crosby take on Danziger for the return from the West Indies? You had a full crew going across, did you not?'

Napley shook his head. 'I don't rightly know why Mr Crosby took him on. We had no trouble outbound; she ran like a bird and we were more than enough to handle her, but when we was in Demerara Mr Crosby said as he thought she was sailing too light, riding too high in the water, like.'

'And he had extra ballast put aboard her?' suggested Holmes.

'That's right, he did. More than I thought was sensible, even if she had been riding light, which I never thought she was. I was quite concerned as she was over-ballasted coming home. I thought she was sluggish and I told Mr Crosby so, but he never paid no mind.'

'And Danziger? What had he to do with all this?'

'I don't rightly know as he did, but Mr Crosby come aboard in Demerara one day and said as he'd found a useful new hand as would make work lighter going home. I don't mind admitting as I was a bit put out. That's a captain's job, that is, taking on of hands, subject, of course, to the owner's agreement, but here was my owner gone over my head and taken on this American.'

'And what has this to do with the ballast?' pressed Holmes.

'Well, I never said nothing to Mr Crosby, but I reckon he knew as I was put out, because it was then he started talking about taking on extra ballast to come home and how the American would be useful on the voyage home.'

'You would have supervised the taking on of the ballast?' asked Holmes.

Napley frowned. 'There again,' he said, 'I should have done, but Mr Crosby, he wouldn't hear of it. He sent me and all the lads off on a trip with a horse and carriage, all expenses paid, and when we come back he and Danziger had put the new ballast aboard.'

'And how did you feel about that, Captain?'

'I was fair unhappy about it, Mr Holmes. After all, I was being paid to sail *Gyrfalcon* and be responsible for her crossing the Atlantic, but here was her owner taking on hands and messing about with her ballast. I tell you, I didn't like it. If aught had happened to us coming home people would have been quick enough to blame me as the captain.'

He paused and refilled his pipe 'But then,' he went on at last, 'Mr Crosby had always been a good owner to work for and I didn't want to lose a good berth, did I? So I held me tongue and when we got home I seen as he agreed with me in the end.'

'How was that?' Holmes asked.

'Well, sir, when we was approaching Plymouth, he said to me as me and the lads had given him a good voyage out and back, and he was pleased, so he was going to land us at Plymouth, and he and Teddy Danziger was going up the Severn to pay calls on some friends of Mr Crosby's, while the rest of us took a train home.'

'Did you know of any of your owner's friends about the Severn?'

'Well, there was people close by Bridgwater he used to visit sometimes and other times he'd go into Penarth.'

'And he and Danziger could have handled *Gyrfalcon*?'

'Oh, yes, sir. Inshore with no heavy weather they'd have had no trouble.'

'So you saw nothing unusual in his suggestion,' said Holmes.

'No, sir. He'd done the same before, only with him and me instead of him and Danziger. When we'd come back from abroad he and me would go somewhere together while the other lads went home.'

'So you came on here,' said Holmes. 'And when did you next see *Gyrfalcon*?'

'About ten days after. She come into the river here, with Mr Crosby and Teddy Danziger working her.'

It was Holmes's turn to refill his pipe. Without looking up from the work of his long fingers he asked, 'And what did you make of the fact that she was much higher in the water?'

'Why,' began the seaman, 'I thought as how . . .' He stopped short, took his pipe from his mouth and stared at my friend. 'Now how on earth did you know that?' he exclaimed. 'I never said nothing about that.'

'Nor did you,' agreed Holmes, 'but what did you make of the fact?'

Napley's eyes never left Holmes. 'Well,' he said, 'I just thought as Mr Crosby had realised the error of his ways, having the handling of the boat himself, like.'

'I see. Tell me, Captain, do you know of Mr Crosby's interest in buried treasure?'

Our guest seemed to have recovered from his surprise, for he chuckled. 'I don't know that it was a very long-lasting thing, sir, but 'tis true as he took a share when the *Alerte* went to Trinidad. That was a few years ago now, eighty-eight or thereabouts. They was going after a great treasure of gold and silver, so it said in the newspapers, but they never found it. When he told me he was going I asked him why he didn't take his own yacht. I said as he'd got a good vessel and a good crew, so why let others take their shares in the prize. He said as he didn't know the exact whereabouts of the treasure, so he'd have to be content with a tenth share.'

'But, in the event, he was prevented by illness from joining in,' said Holmes.

'That's right, sir. Two days only before they was to sail, Mr Crosby come down with the flu, so he couldn't go.' He drew thoughtfully at his pipe. 'But they never found nothing, anyhow.'

Holmes nodded. 'So you were working for Mr Crosby then, in eighty-eight?'

'Oh, yes, sir. He took me on as his captain when he first had *Esmerelde*. She was a tough boat, sir. You had to work hard to make her fly, but we done it. We went deep ocean with her more than a few times and we won the Enticott Cup in ninety-two. Then Mr Crosby sold her, after the Cup, to an American gent, and then he had *Gyrfalcon* built.'

'So you are *Gyrfalcon*'s first and only skipper,' said Holmes.

'That's right, sir.'

'Do you think, Captain, that you would recognise *Gyrfalcon* if, say, she were to be repainted, renamed, perhaps had her sails changed?'

'Recognise her, Mr Holmes? Why, of course I would! I watched her being built, you know, and I've sailed her ever since. It would take more than a dab of paint and a new suit of sails to hide *Gyrfalcon* from me. As to her name, well I never looks at a boat's name, not till I've looked her over to see if I know her cut.'

Holmes reached into his pocket and pulled out a small handful of sovereigns. Placing them on the table, he said, 'You have offered to help Mrs Crosby. Take this for your expenses and look for *Gyrfalcon* for me, will you?'

'I'd be glad to, sir, but where should I start to look?'

'I leave that to you, Captain Napley. You know the yachting harbours and their people. Go where you think *Gyrfalcon* may be. If you run short of money, wire me in London and I shall send more.'

'What if she's abroad?' Napley asked.

Holmes shook his head. 'She is not. Danziger left his lodgings with Mr Crosby, saying that he would be away for a few days only. At best he was only crossing the Channel, but Scotland Yard have circularised the continental ports, as well as the British harbours on the south and east coasts. She is laid up in some unusual harbour where yachts do not normally ply, I'll be bound. What is more, I am sure that you are the one man who can find her fast, Captain.'

Napley pocketed the little pile of coins. 'Aye, aye, Mr Holmes,' he said.

Chapter Seven

A Message at Twilight

His business with Napley done, Holmes asked the Captain to take us to Morris's yard and introduce us. The yachtsman led us from the Boatman's Arms, along the quayside, to where a green and gold painted board proclaimed 'E. and A. Morris, All Manner of Vessels Repaired and Maintained, Chandlery and Riverage, Boats for Hire' at the entrance between two high wooden fences. Once through the gate, we were among cut timber, stacked timber and great balks lying in open-sided sheds, filling the warm afternoon with their pungent scents. The shifting note of a mechanical saw sang out regularly from somewhere behind a shed and the sound of hammers echoed in short bursts.

Mr Morris emerged from the gloom of one of his sheds and came to meet us, a short, plump man, with weather-beaten features and pale-blue eyes, clad in overalls liberally dashed with glue and varnish, topped by a battered marine cap. Once we had been introduced by Captain Napley, the yard's master led us up a wooden outside stairway into a long gloomy loft. Here masts and spars lay on trestles, and coils of rope and line were heaped about, while festoons of sails hung from the rafters. At the far end he showed us into a small office, its desk stacked with constructional drawings and every available inch of wall covered with photographs of yachts.

He waved us to the only three chairs in the room and perched himself on the corner of a large tool chest, pulling a stubby pipe from his pocket and shouting through the open door for four mugs of tea.

Until we were served, Morris and Napley chatted about the weather and regatta prospects, but at last a fresh-faced youth in overalls arrived with enamel mugs of sweet orange tea.

'Now then, gentlemen,' Morris enquired, after a long pull at his mug. 'What can I do for you?'

'You might tell us', said Holmes, 'what you know about Mr Crosby's *Gyrfalcon*.'

'Ah, *Gyrfalcon*. Well, sir, I had *Esmerelde* first, ever since Mr Crosby bought her. Then when he sold her he brought *Gyrfalcon* here as soon as she was built and he always kept her here when he wasn't at the regattas or cruising.'

'And did he often go cruising?' asked Holmes.

'Well, sir, once the regattas was over he'd often go foreign, over to France or down to the Med, but a few times he took her over to America, didn't he, Jim?' he appealed to Napley.

Napley nodded. 'We was four times across the Atlantic,' he confirmed. 'Most times just to New England. This last time was longest, over to Maine, then down to the West Indies before coming home.'

'He had never visited the West Indies before?' Holmes enquired.

'Not while I skippered for him,' said Napley, 'and I never heard him say as he knew the place.'

'Were you surprised', Holmes asked Morris, 'when

51

Gyrfalcon came in with only Mr Crosby and one hand?'

Morris shook his head 'No, sir,' he said, ''cos Jim here and his crew had come home and said as Mr Crosby and the American had taken *Gyrfalcon* up the Severn, and anyway, I always expected *Gyrfalcon* in just before the regattas so as I could see to any bits and bobs that wanted doing to her.'

'And what was her condition when she came in?'

'Well, she been across the Atlantic twice and down to the West Indies. There was bound to be a bit of wear, but nothing serious. The worst was a long scrape on her port side, but 'twas only a paint and varnish job.'

'What do you think caused that?' asked my friend.

Morris sucked at his pipe. 'I did wonder about that,' he admitted. 'It was too long to be done by another vessel.'

'Why is that?' said Holmes.

'Well, sir,' Morris answered, 'a boat or a ship is all curves, sir. She curves from bow to stern and she curves downwards to the keel. That means as when two vessels strike each other, even if one of them slides alongside the other, there isn't that much contact between them to make a long scrape. A long scrape'll only come from hitting something flattish, and usually something as isn't moving.'

'So how did you think *Gyrfalcon* had been injured, Mr Morris?'

'Well, the most likely thing is scraping up against a wall.'

'I take it', Holmes said to Napley, 'that there was no such mark on her when you brought her into Plymouth?'

'None at all, Mr Holmes. It must have been done up the Severn.'

'If that is, indeed, where they went,' murmured Holmes. 'You might add to my instructions to you,

Captain, a request to visit the Severn harbours which you have visited with Mr Crosby and see if *Gyrfalcon* has been seen in any of them.'

He turned again to Morris. 'What did you make', he asked, 'of the fact that she was lighter in the water than when you last saw her?'

'Why, I seen that as soon as she come up the river. Soon as Mr Crosby was ashore I told him as she was riding too high and needed more ballast.'

'What did he say?'

'He said as he thought she'd handle better in the ocean, so he'd dropped some of her ballast in Demerara.'

'But that's not true!' exclaimed Napley. 'He didn't take any out – he put more in at Demerara!'

'Well, Jim, that's what he told me. Asked me to top her up the way she was before.'

'Does either of you know', asked my friend, 'from which direction *Gyrfalcon* came to Eacham on her last call?'

'From which direction?' Morris sounded puzzled. 'There's only one way, up Southampton Water and into the river.'

'I apologise, Mr Morris. I expressed myself badly. I was referring to the direction from which she approached the mouth of Southampton Water.'

Napley shook his head, but Morris said, 'Yes, I can tell you that. Mr Anderson had taken his *Freebooter* off me that I'd been working on and he took her down the water to give her a run in the open sea. He came in and said as he'd passed *Gyrfalcon* just west of Hurst Castle, coming from Plymouth.'

'So, if she was west of Hurst Castle, they hadn't been in the Hamble,' stated Holmes.

'No, no, we should have heard if they was that close,' said Morris.

'So, when she came in, what did Mr Crosby require of you?' asked Holmes.

'Well, sir, apart from the ballasting, he wanted me to see as she was all shipshape for the season, just as I was expecting he would want.'

'And she moored out in the river?'

'That's right. What with the regattas coming, I had a good few boats about the jetties, so Mr Crosby moored her out there at the buoy.' He pointed through a dusty window that overlooked the estuary.

'I see,' said Holmes, 'and what happened on the Saturday evening when the American took her out again?'

'Ah, you'd best ask old Pally about that, sir.' Morris got up and went to the office door, shouting into the echoing loft, 'Brian! Do you fetch old Pally out of the Boatman's and tell him there's gentlemen here about *Gyrfalcon* as wants a word with him.'

Pally Usher was soon with us, a short, slight man with nervous dark eyes sunk in a flushed face. A woollen cap was pulled tightly down over his brows and, despite the warmth of the afternoon, he was clad in a cast-off naval overcoat that fell nearly to his ankles. A luxurious grey beard and moustache partly concealed a mouthful of stained teeth.

Entering the little office, he snatched off his cap and clutched it with both hands, as though approaching the quarterdeck.

'Now, Pally,' said Morris, 'these here gentlemen are looking into the disappearance of *Gyrfalcon* and I've told them as you're the man who can tell them what happened that night.'

The quaint little man nodded silently and Morris turned to us. 'There'd been a bit of thieving going on,' he explained. 'Well, there's always a bit going on in a boatyard. People takes home a dab of paint or a bit of timber as'll serve some purpose and I never makes no mind, but it had gotten out of hand. There was fresh pots of paint and varnish going, and lanterns and tools, and once even a big balk of timber. There were a lot of boats in at the time, not just here at my moorings, but along the river, and I had my suspicions of some of them, but I couldn't prove nothing, so I set old Pally here to watch for them at night. That's what he was doing when he saw *Gyrfalcon* going out.'

'From where were you keeping watch?' Holmes asked the little man.

'I were on the *Kingfisher*,' he said. 'That's the steam launch that's still there at the north jetty. I thought as if I stayed on the *Kingfisher* I should see anyone as came or went from the yard, and they most likely wouldn't see me 'cos they wouldn't expect no one to be on board her at night.' He smiled, pleased with his own cunning.

'And what first alerted you?' asked Holmes.

'Well, sir, it were late on – a good while after the Boatman's closed – and I heard footsteps coming along the quay. I looked over *Kingfisher*'s stern and I could see someone walking down the quay past the Boatman's.'

'Could you see who it was?' Holmes enquired.

'Oh, yes, sir. Soon as saw him, I knowed who it was. It was Teddy Danziger as crewed for Mr Crosby. I could tell by his size and him limping on the left side.'

'And what did you do?'

'Well, I kept watching, making sure as he wouldn't see me. See, I thought he might be the one that'd been in Mr Morris's yard, so I watched him coming along, but he didn't come down here to the yard, he went out on the south jetty and jumped down into a boat. Now I couldn't see what he was about down there, but soon he had the boat out on the water and he was pulling out where *Gyrfalcon* was moored, out at the buoy. Well, I didn't think nothing about that, you see, 'cos I knew he was crew on *Gyrfalcon* and I just reckoned as he'd got nowhere to sleep and was going to sleep aboard, you see.'

'And what happened then?' my friend pursued.

'Well, like I say, I thought he wasn't the one as I was watching for, so I didn't pay much mind. I carried on keeping my eye about the quayside, but then I heard noises from *Gyrfalcon* and I looked out. I saw as he'd tied the rowboat to the buoy and he was on *Gyrfalcon*, putting her sail up and getting weigh on her, and sure enough, she went quietly away down the river while I watched her.'

'And you are certain that it was the American – Teddy Danziger – that you saw take her out?'

'Certain sure,' he said.

'It must have been dark,' pressed Holmes.

The little man stood his ground. 'Not so dark as all that, sir. There was a fair bit of moon and anyway, like I said, sir, I knowed him before I could rightly see him, by that limping step of his.'

'And how well did you know Danziger?' asked Holmes. 'After all, he had not been long in Eacham.'

'Nor had he, sir, but 'tain't a big place, like. I seed him most every day in the Boatman's and more than once he bought me a pint.'

'Then I can do no less,' Holmes smiled and passed Usher a coin. The little fellow knuckled his forelock, crammed on his woollen cap and scuttled away along the loft.

'Well, gentlemen,' said Holmes, 'I think we can be sure that it was the American who took *Gyrfalcon* out. It remains for you, Captain Napley, to find where he took her.'

We dined that evening at the Boatman's Arms, where Holmes had elected to stay overnight. After dark he surprised me by suggesting a stroll on the quayside.

'A constitutional, Holmes?' I queried.

'Certainly not,' he replied. 'A small piece of research. We cannot have the light exactly as it was, but let us find out if we can satisfy ourselves as to how well Usher could see.'

We strolled along the quayside towards the north jetty, where the gleaming steam launch *Kingfisher* was still moored. Holmes scrambled aboard her and I followed. For several minutes my friend peered silently about him, up the quayside towards the inn and out across the estuary to the mooring buoy, without comment.

It was nearly sunset and the dying sun shot a handful of beams through the trees across the river, streaking the water with light and striking bright golden sparks from the occasional ripples. Suddenly I glimpsed a flicker of something, caught by a ray of the sun as it flew over the water. For an instant I thought it was a kingfisher, swooping to take the evening insects that hung above the water, then I realised that it lacked the gaudy colours of that lovely bird. It takes far longer to write than it took my soldierly instincts to operate. I flung myself behind *Kingfisher*'s bulwark and jerked Holmes down beside me.

'Watson!' he exclaimed, but he got no further before something struck the upright supporting *Kingfisher*'s awning, against which my friend had been leaning. It was a full yard long and its point buried itself deeply in the varnished post – an arrow fired from the darkness across the river.

Chapter Eight

Sherlock Holmes Theorises

It is more than fifteen years since I soldiered in the bandit-haunted passes of Afghanistan, but I thanked heaven that the protective instincts I developed then had not deserted me and, if my brain was slow to recognise an arrow flying in the twilight, my muscles had not lost their reaction. I sat on *Kingfisher*'s deck and tremblingly lit a cigarette, conscious of our narrow escape.

'If you have done with that match, Watson, be a good fellow and hold it up here,' said Holmes. He had his pocket knife out and was carefully cutting the weapon's head out of the woodwork.

'Get down, Holmes!' I hissed.

'Nonsense,' he responded. 'Whoever fired that arrow will be long gone. Our voices will have carried across the water and he knows that he missed. He won't try again now.'

He had the weapon's point freed and, lighting one of the launch's lanterns, he held the implement up to the light. It was made from about a yard of a stout dried reed of some kind and triple-feathered. There was no marking or binding on its shaft, but the head was an inch and a quarter of quartz shaped into a deadly tri-angular blade.

'Have you seen such a thing before, Watson?' Holmes asked.

I shook my head. 'I have seen arrows tipped with stone and with metal,' I said, 'but I do not recall coming across one tipped with quartz.'

'Nor I. Tomorrow I shall have to seek expert advice when we return to London.'

Dousing the lantern, we made our way back to our lodgings and I admit that my shoulders felt uneasy until the solid oak door of the inn closed behind us.

On our journey back to London in the morning Holmes was in high good humour.

'You consider our trip a success, then?' I asked.

'Oh, indeed, Watson, indeed. We have learned more of Crosby than Lestrade told us. We have confirmed that Danziger moved *Gyrfalcon* We have a reasonable theory – though it is only a theory – as to the cause of this whole curious affair and we have further evidence as to the identity of the person who may well be Crosby's murderer.'

I was dumbfounded. 'Really!' I exclaimed. 'Are you not in danger of breaking your own rule and theorising before possessing all the facts?'

'Certainly not,' he snapped. 'I have told you before, Watson, that it is perfectly permissible to extrapolate theories from the known facts so long as those theories do not conflict with the facts or with common sense.'

'Then what theories have you?' I asked.

'Consider,' he said and leaned forward on the train's seat, striking off his points with one finger of his right hand on the fingers of the other. 'First, Crosby was in financial difficulties and had been for some time.'

'But his widow said that he had made more than ample provision for her and his children,' I protested.

'Oh, indeed, Watson, but only lately and from a source which she does not know. Second, he was a racing yachtsman, racing for prizes, and that aspect of his personality extended to the possibility of searching for treasure.'

'But he didn't go with the *Alerte*,' I contradicted.

'Do try to confine yourself to what is relevant, Watson. If he had not been prevented by influenza he would have gone. That is what matters. Third, he took on in Demerara an entirely supernumerary addition to his regular crew – Teddy Danziger. Fourth, after taking on the American he increased *Gyrfalcon*'s ballast . . .'

'I confess I do not understand all that toing and froing about the ballast,' I interrupted. 'Surely, that was just a difference of opinion between master and skipper that put Napley's nose out of joint?'

Holmes snorted. 'Watson, it is in the manoeuvring with *Gyrfalcon*'s ballast that one can see the dim shape of a solution. She went foreign with her usual ballast. That will have been some tons of lead, stowed in the space beneath her floorboards, apart from some attached to her keel.'

'Right,' I conceded.

'Napley made no mention of her misbehaving on the outward voyage, yet Crosby decided at Demerara – after signing Danziger – that her ballast needed increasing. What is more, he ensured that his regular crew took no part in the shipping of the additional ballast.'

'I thought that was a bit suspicious,' I admitted.

'Marvellous, Watson. Can you not see that the entire transaction is suspicious? *Gyrfalcon* returned from the West Indies with the heavier ballast and, on making Plymouth, Crosby released his regular crew and set off somewhere with Danziger. When she shows up in the Itchen, she is sailing light, having disposed of that extra ballast somewhere – somewhere, perhaps, unfamiliar to Crosby, where he scraped her port side badly.'

He looked at me expectantly, but I was still unable to make the connections that he seemed to think were obvious. 'I'm sorry,' I said. 'I am still all at sea.'

He snorted again. 'Taken with the sudden increase in Crosby's funds, I cannot escape the inference that Danziger, learning that Crosby was returning to England and maybe that he was a commercial banker to boot, propositioned Crosby to carry a heavy and valuable cargo across the Atlantic in the guise of ballast. How better to ship something of dubious provenance into the country? What Customs official is going to bother the wealthy owner of a racing yacht? On arrival at Plymouth, that cargo was taken elsewhere and unshipped, the proceeds of the operation ending up in Crosby's account. Crosby, apart from being short of funds, was exactly the kind of man who would fall in with such a scheme – one that smelled of adventure and profit.' He sat back with a triumphant expression.

'Yes,' I agreed, 'I can see that makes sense. But what do you believe they shipped in *Gyrfalcon*?'

'If I were in the habit of guessing, Watson, I would say that their ballast consisted of precious metal in some shape or form, but it is only important for one reason.'

'What is that?'

'Because someone evidently takes strong exception to their operation, whether the acquisition of whatever they carried or the shipping of it to England. Someone has pursued them, captured and tortured poor Crosby, executed him and published his deed by sending the head to the Yard.'

'You said you had some information as to that person's identity I reminded him.'

'So I have, Watson. In the first place there is the extremely able burglar who invaded Danziger's London lodging. I think we may speculate that our burglar is the same foreign person who called on Mr Graby enquiring for Danziger. He is either the person who has taken exception to Crosby and Danziger bringing whatever they brought to England, or he is an agent of that person.'

'But how have you derived more information about him while we were at Eacham?' I asked.

'The arrow, Watson, the arrow! It is a distinctive weapon and I have great hopes that a suitable expert may be able to tell us whence it originates.'

He would make no further comment on the matter, leaving me to mull over his points while he discoursed about execution rituals in the Dark Ages and the proper pronunciation of Latin.

He separated from me at Waterloo, leaving me to ferry our bags to Baker Street while he took the arrow and disappeared in the direction of the British Museum.

I had given up waiting for him and instructed Mrs Hudson to lay tea, when his footstep sounded on the stair. He strode in, pitched his hat on the rack and fell into an armchair, dropping the arrow on the table to the disgruntlement of our landlady. 'Ah, tea!' he exclaimed. 'I confess that when I visit the British Museum I realise why study is said to be a dry pursuit.'

'I shall be pleased to serve your tea, Mr Holmes, if you will be good enough to remove this – this thing, whatever it is, from the tea table,' said Mrs Hudson.

He leaned across and snatched the arrow. 'This thing, whatever it is,' he repeated. 'There is the nub of the question. From where would you say this implement originated, Watson?'

I took it from him and examined it closely. It told me no more than it had done under *Kingfisher*'s lantern the night before. 'I can make nothing of the object itself,' I admitted, 'other than the fact that it is an arrow. I imagine if I were pressed I might suggest that it came from somewhere in the Caribbean, but that is only because of Crosby's calling there. I had thought that the Carib Indians were long suppressed.'

'You make one connection, but not another,' Holmes said. 'Have you not forgotten an American, a native of

Arizona, who wears Western riding boots and displays a considerable talent with a Colt revolver?'

I stared at him. 'You mean . . .' I began.

'Yes, Watson. Where you find a cowboy it is not unreasonable to look for an Indian, surely, and we have found one. Mr Spendlove at the Museum has assured me that a triple-feathered arrow, made from a reed and tipped with a triangular quartz point can only have originated from the redskin tribe known to their enemies as the Apache.'

'Good heavens!' I exclaimed. 'How comes Crosby to be involved in the affairs of some retired Arizona pistoleer and a tribe of savage Indians?'

'We shall discover that in due course,' he said with assurance. 'I hazard the suggestion that whatever valuables Crosby brought to England in *Gyrfalcon* may be some kind of tribal property. That would account for the pursuit, its ruthless nature and the ritual aspect of the banker's death, would it not?'

Mrs Hudson had finished at the table and we took our places. A faint bell of recollection rang at the back of my mind while we ate, but it took a while to make itself clear. 'Holmes,' I said, 'your man at the Museum is quite sure that this is an Apache arrow?'

'Quite sure,' he replied. 'The reed shaft, the triple feather and the quartz head all confirm its origin. Why do you ask?'

'I only caught a glimpse of that curious document which Mrs Crosby placed in your keeping,' I went on, 'but was not the word "Apache" written on it?'

'So it was, Watson, so it was. I must give you full marks. Not content with saving my life last night, you have now pointed out a connection I had overlooked. Once tea is done I must send a telegram, after which we might profitably, I believe, apply our wits to that document.'

Chapter Nine

Words and Pictures

As Mrs Hudson cleared away our meal, Holmes scribbled a telegram and gave it to her for the boy to send. Then he extracted Crosby's document from his writing desk and laid it on the table.

I had seen it but briefly when the banker's widow had handed it to my friend and had only remarked that it was a list of words, each followed by a symbol of some kind. Now I could see that neither the words nor the symbols seemed to bear much connection between themselves or with each other.

The words were SUPERSTITIONS, followed by a skull and crossbones, BARK, followed by a flower-like symbol or a symbol for the sun, SILVER and KING, each followed by a six-pointed star, SUPERIOR, followed by an ornamental cross, NEEDLE, followed by a lozenge shape, DOOR, followed by a lozenge divided into four parts, JUNCTION, followed by a square with a loop at each corner, WEAVERS, with the plain lozenge. APACHE, with the looped square, PERALTA, with a box containing a Saint Andrew's Cross, GREEN and SPRING, each with two ragged parallel lines, and BOX and CANON, both with a plain square.

I shook my head over it. 'You have always advised me to seek for patterns, but I see none here, apart from the repetition of some of the symbols.'

'Then let us take note of that fact,' said Holmes and, taking a piece of paper, he rewrote the list in three columns:

SUPERSTITIONS	SILVER	KING
BARK	NEEDLE	WEAVERS
SUPERIOR	JUNCTION	APACHE
DOOR	GREEN	SPRING
PERALTA	BOX	CANON

'There. The first column contains words identified with only one symbol, the second and third contain the pairs identified by duplication of a symbol. Does that assist us?'

'It reveals that there are ten words with one symbol and ten words shared between the pairs,' I observed.

'So it does,' he agreed, 'though I cannot see why that should be significant. What of the words themselves?'

He ran his pencil point lightly down the list. 'There are twelve nouns,' he announced, 'two of them plural, plus the adjectives GREEN and SUPERIOR and this strange word PERALTA. It does not help that BARK and SPRING may also be verbs, as may NEEDLE, and that APACHE occurs both in American English and in French with different meanings.' Silently, he looked again at the lists.

'Might it not be possible', I suggested, 'to associate each word in some way with the symbol which follows it?'

'It is easy to associate SUPERSTITIONS with the skull and bones,' he said. 'Many superstitions are connected with death, but what of the symbol following BARK? Is it a flower? Is it the sun? Whichever, what is the connection with BARK? And is it the bark of a tree, the bark of a dog, the bark which injures or the bark which sails?'

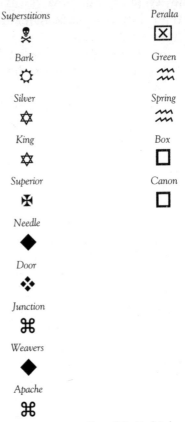

Copy of Mrs Crosby's document

'There seems to be a connection between KING and SILVER and the six-pointed star,' I said. 'The symbol is known as the Star of King David and is reproduced in silver as an ornament.'

'What, then, do you make of NEEDLE and WEAVERS,' he asked. 'The lozenge most famously appears as the diamond on a pack of cards, but we have no spade, heart or club, and no apparent link between playing cards and needles or weavers.'

'What about GREEN and SPRING?' I asked.

66

'What of them, Watson? Spring is the green season, if that is what you mean, but how does that connect to the symbol?'

'You pointed out', I said, 'that several of these words have more than one meaning. Now spring is the green season, which associates it with the word bearing the same symbol, but it is also a source of water. Does not the symbol suggest water?'

'Spring also means "leap", Watson, and I think you are leaping at unworkable associations. By your theory, what would you make of BOX and CANON? The symbol may well be a symbol for a box, but it is not a symbol for a canon, nor is there any obvious association between the two words.'

'Canon is easily misspelt,' I suggested.

'Nor is a square a recognisable symbol for the other variety of cannon, Watson. The associations between the pairs of words which have the same symbol must be made by something other than their common meaning.'

'There is a play called *The Silver King*,' I said. 'We have seen it.'

'So there is,' he agreed, 'but what help is that? I see no *Hamlet* here, no *Bells* here, no *Macbeth*, no *Ticket of Leave Man*. I do not think we are dealing with the titles of popular dramas.'

'Then I am at a loss,' I admitted.

'No more than I am, Watson.' He scanned the list again, shaking his head. 'They are all common words, apart from Apache, which has two meanings, and PER-ALTA, which means nothing to me.'

'What about', I suggested, 'the three words which have a lozenge after them – NEEDLE with a lozenge, DOOR with a divided lozenge and WEAVERS with a whole lozenge?'

He gazed at me without comment.

'What I had in mind', I explained, 'was to find a triple association which combines the three words, but distinguishes DOOR in some way.'

'Very cunning, Watson,' he said. 'Have you any connections in mind?'

'Do not weavers employ needles?' I wondered.

'No, Watson. Seamstresses and knitters employ needles. Weavers employ shuttles. On the other hand, weavers do employ doors, but so do kings and Apaches, not to mention thousands of persons and professions who are not listed here. Perhaps even peraltas do – whatever they may be!'

'It sounds Latin,' I said, 'Spanish or Portuguese, or maybe Italian.'

'I do believe that to be the first practical suggestion that you have made, Watson.' he muttered and, getting up from the table, approached the bookshelves.

His long fingers wandered along the rows of books, pausing here and there to draw one out. He would flip through its pages, close it with a snap and thrust it back into its place, before seeking another. At last he returned to the table. 'There is no such name in any encyclopaedia,' he said, 'but you may still be right. I have an uneasy feeling that it is a name and one which I have seen in some connection.'

I had been poring over the list while Holmes sought a reference in the bookshelves.

'Look,' I said, 'many of these words might be names. Apache, we know, is the name of an Indian tribe. Peralta might be an Italian or Spanish name, but a lot of the others – bark, king, silver, weaver, green, spring and box – might be English surnames.'

He looked doubtful, but he checked the list again. 'What you say is true, Watson, but what significance would it have? If Crosby or Danziger wished to preserve a list of names, they would be safer in a cipher than simply disguised as ordinary words. What, also, would you make of the other words, let alone the symbols?'

'Perhaps', I hazarded, 'they are persons who have some kind of interest in whatever valuable property Crosby and Danziger transported from Demerara.

Maybe the symbols indicate the nature of their interest, or show what sort of person they are.'

'You are stretching a slender idea transparently thin, Watson. I repeat that such a list would be better concealed by a cipher known only to Crosby and Danziger.'

I was crestfallen. For a short time I had believed that I had succeeded in making a connection between most of the words on the list that Holmes had not seen. 'If you would be so kind as to jot down a copy of the list,' I said, 'I will take a stroll in the park. Who knows, the fresh air might produce an inspiration.'

He rapidly copied the list and passed me the copy. 'In your absence,' he said, 'I shall treat this as at the least a three-pipe problem.'

The summer evening was delightful and, after a stroll, I settled on a bench in the park with my copy of the list and a box of cigarettes; but the consumption of several cigarettes led me no further into the mysterious document and the evening turned unseasonably chilly. At last I conceded defeat and retraced my steps to Baker Street.

Holmes, when I returned, was squatting cross-legged atop a mound of cushions on the couch, his eyes closed, his pipe in his mouth and the sitting room blue with smoke. 'Watson!' he greeted me. 'Has a turn in the park revealed all to you?'

'No,' I admitted, 'and I take it that your own attempts are no further forward.'

He drew deeply on his pipe. 'They are certainly not fruitful, in the sense that I still do not know what the document means, but I am beginning to develop an idea about its nature.'

'Really?'

He nodded. 'It occurs to me', he said, 'that our list is, in itself, a key of some kind.'

'A key?' I asked, puzzled.

'Yes. I believe that it reveals nothing because one or more important elements are absent. Suppose, for example, that there were a second list, in which other words were followed by the same symbols. That would create the possibility of meaningful conjunctions between pairs of words, instead of the seemingly senseless pairings that emerge from this list.'

'Yes,' I said slowly. 'Then the keeping of the two lists separately would achieve greater security than maintaining the two as one document? Is that what you have in mind?'

'Something along those lines,' he agreed, 'though I postulate the existence of a second, different, list merely as an example. Nor need it be only one element that is absent. It might be two or more.'

'Holmes,' I complained, 'your partial solution bids fair to make the whole thing impossible! Apart from which, where are we to find the second or other elements of the puzzle?'

'Crosby had this part,' he said. 'It would seem reasonable to believe that Danziger had the other, if there are only two.'

'And where did he keep it? It was not in his lodgings,' I pointed out.

'No, indeed. It might still be with him, aboard *Gyrfalcon*, assuming for the moment that he is aboard the yacht. Even if he is not, the other part of our puzzle may be aboard her.'

'Then we must wait until we hear from Captain Napley,' I said.

'I merely expressed a theory, Watson. I do not intend to stop trying to unravel this singular document, but I shall not be entirely surprised if we do need Napley's information or some other connection made before we can see the significance of the list.'

Chapter Ten

A Visitor by Night

I had offered Holmes all the ideas and opinions that had occurred to me in connection with Crosby's list and I was, at first, delighted when he suggested that perhaps it could not be solved without some further information. However, so far from breaking off his own attempts to decipher the document, he remained squatting on his mound of cushions, his eyes partly closed and his pipe glowing like a blast furnace.

'Holmes,' I said, after more than an hour, 'if it cannot be solved without some key, which we do not have, what is the point of continuing to try?'

'The point, Watson, lies in two facts. One is that it is merely a theory of mine that some further data is required to unlock the secrets of this list, and I could conceivably be in error; the second is that, if I am correct, it may be possible to infer the nature of the missing data from the present list.'

'I do not see how,' I demurred.

'I have told you often, Watson, that it is theoretically possible to infer the existence of an ocean from a grain of sand.'

'So you have,' I agreed, 'but you have never completely convinced me.'

He smiled disarmingly. 'Then let me limit my analogies to the more prosaic. Would you agree that it is possible to infer the nature of a key from the nature of its lock?'

I hesitated, sensing that he was seeking to persuade me against my will.

'Come, Watson,' he urged. 'If it were not possible, no locksmith would be able to replace a lost key.'

'But a locksmith does that by examining and measuring the lock, assessing its method of operation and deducing what manner of key of what size will both fit the lock and operate it,' I protested.

'Precisely.' He smiled. 'Now here we have a lock, I suspect, and I am merely examining it in the hope of discovering its mechanism. If I succeed then it will be that much easier to recognise the appropriate key when I see it.'

There were often times when Holmes's arguments about the nature of deduction and analysis struck me as purely theoretical, indeed, far-fetched, and this was one of them.

I selected a novel from the bookshelves. 'It is beyond me,' I said. 'I wish you joy of it.' And I bade him a good night.

In the event I did not enjoy a good night myself. While my choice of reading was sufficiently dull to send me rapidly to sleep, the summer night had turned cold. Several times I half woke, chilly and aware that my dreams had been invaded by words and images from Crosby's list. I was glad when the rattle of the morning traffic on Baker Street woke me for the last time and gave me an excuse to rise.

I was pleased, also, on entering the sitting room, to

find that Holmes had not, as he often did, spent the entire night there, wrestling with his problem. Although the whole room was thick with pipe smoke, I could detect that it was all of some staleness. At some point in the night my friend had abandoned his efforts and sought his bed. It crossed my mind that he might have succeeded in wresting a meaning from the list, but despite my admiration for his intellectual powers I doubted it.

I was, therefore, the more surprised when Holmes entered, just as I was making for the window with a view to relieving the room's fug.

'Good morning, Watson,' he said. 'You are about early.'

'No more so than you,' I countered. 'When I left you last night I would have bet on you spending all night squatting on the couch.'

He smiled. 'I spent a good part of the night in that fashion, but I made no progress, so I accepted your argument and went to bed.'

I opened a window slightly, but not too far, for it was still fresh.

Holmes seated himself at the table. 'Watson,' he said suddenly, 'has Mrs Hudson been about yet?'

I shook my head. 'I very much doubt it,' I said. 'When I came down, the room was still full of your tobacco smoke and the cushions still heaped on the sofa. I don't think she'd have let those pass.'

'No indeed,' he agreed. 'Tell me, then. Before I joined you this morning had you any occasion to move the vase on the table by the window?'

'No,' I answered, perplexed. 'I was barely in the room before you came in. What is the matter with the vase?'

Our landlady, in one of her persistent efforts to soften our masculine sitting room, had recently placed a large vase of mixed flowers on the table that stood immediately in front of the windows. It stood there still, though I noted that the flowers had suffered more than a little from Holmes's pipe.

'You did not move the vase when you opened the window?' he asked.

'No,' I confirmed. 'Holmes, what concerns you about the vase?'

'Merely that it is not in its accustomed place on the table. It has been moved to one side.'

'But it might have been moved yesterday,' I said.

'So it might, Watson, but it was not. When I retired in the small hours it was still placed centrally on its table. Now it is towards the left-hand edge. If Mrs Hudson has not been in and you have not moved it, Watson, there is only one explanation which meets the facts.'

'What is that?'

'We have been burgled during the night, Watson.'

'Surely not,' I exclaimed.

'Why not?' he asked. 'I have long thought that the façades of these houses seem to be designed especially to assist the burglar. Our front doorway is surrounded by stones, which stand out alternately, providing a ladder to the top of the ground floor. The blind fittings of the shop below would provide a reasonable footing after that, and it would be a simple matter to swing over that ridiculous iron rail across this floor and gain access to the windows.'

He stood up and strode across to the window, examining the catch with care. 'Ha!' he exclaimed after a moment. 'I thought as much. We have been visited by the same gentleman who called on Danziger. He has forced our window catch in the same way. Certainly our frontage would present no obstacles to a man who could climb that rear drainpipe at Graby's shop.'

'But what has the vase to do with it?' I enquired.

'Simply that, in climbing through the window, he

moved the vase aside so as to step down on to the table top and forgot to replace it in leaving.'

I looked around our cluttered room. 'But why would he break in here? Has anything been taken?'

Holmes had his lens in hand and was carefully examining the surface of the table under the window. He ignored my question, but beckoned me across. 'Look,' he said, pointing to the table top. 'I had thought that Mrs Hudson's standards of housekeeping would have permitted him to leave less evidence than he did at Graby's, but I was wrong. See? In the waxen polish of the table top, that singular pattern we observed at Graby's.'

I peered closely and could, indeed, see an oval mark impressed upon the polished surface. It appeared to have been made by a pad of coarse cloth. 'He stepped there,' I said, 'wearing those curious cloth pads on his feet.'

'Exactly, Watson!' Holmes agreed.

'Do you know, Holmes,' I added, 'I have remembered where I have heard of something similar.'

'Really?'

'Yes. When I was a boy in Australia I heard that the Kadaitcha men – the witch doctors of the aboriginal tribes – wear boots made of feathers when they set out to kill someone, so that they will leave no trail.'

'Really?' he repeated. 'Well, that is undoubtedly the intent here, but I think we may safely say that there is no reason to believe that there is an Australian element in our little puzzle.'

I stood, looking round the room in a vain effort to determine if anything had been stolen. The clutter of books, papers, chemical equipment and souvenirs defeated me.

'Watson,' Holmes said. 'You will, I think, be of greater assistance to me if you will put yourself in the basket chair and remain there until I have completed my survey of the room.'

I did as he asked and he stalked about the room, his eyes peering in this direction and that. I wondered if it was possible that he really held in his memory the presence and position of every item in our crowded sitting room. I lit a cigarette and let my own eyes scan the room. I had surveyed all four walls, without any certainty as to whether any item was missing, and had let my eyes drop towards the floor.

Opposite me, across the hearth, was the brass coal scuttle, in which it was Holmes's whim to store his cigars and cheroots. At first I thought that the container had been disturbed and a cigar had dropped out on to the carpet, then I realised what it was that I saw.

'Holmes!' I hissed and pointed urgently to the coal scuttle.

He had been standing by his writing desk. Now he whirled about and his eyes followed my pointing finger.

'Upon my word!' he said softly. 'That is why he came. Pray remain still and silent, Watson.'

I had no intention of moving, for protruding from the dark mouth of the coal scuttle were the head of a large snake and a few inches of its body.

Holmes reached behind him and grasped a cylindrical ebony rule on the writing desk. 'It cannot see, Watson, but it can hear,' he said quietly. 'Do you think you could lean across and drop some small change on top of the coal scuttle?'

Without taking my eyes off the snake, I drew a few small coins from my pocket and, leaning across the fireplace, dropped them on to the coal scuttle.

The sudden rattle of the falling coins produced an immediate effect. The creature's head lifted and swung from side to side, its tongue flickering in and out of its mouth, while from within the coal scuttle came a muffled whirring noise.

As its head swung back towards me, Holmes took a silent pace forward and flung a bunch of keys from his pocket on to the floor beside the serpent. Quick as lightning its head flashed back towards the keys and, in the same moment, Holmes struck it a powerful blow behind the head with the ebony ruler, holding the weapon down at the end of the blow and forcing the creature's head into the fireside rug.

The snake writhed a time or two after Holmes's attack, but soon it went limp. Holmes drew the body of the thing out of the coal scuttle. It was longer than either of our British snakes and its back bore a bold pattern of lozenges, while its tail was tipped with the unmistakable rings of the American rattlesnake. Holmes doubled the snake in two along the top of his writing desk. 'Unless I am mistaken,' he remarked, 'this is a diamond-backed rattlesnake, a native of the south-western areas of the United States. I think we may count ourselves lucky that last night was not as warm as some have been recently. Our burglar having left us this unpleasant surprise, the chilly night caused it to seek shelter and made it drowsy. I cannot say that I like to dwell on the possibilities of it roaming this room on a warm morning.'

There was a tap at the door and Holmes quickly closed the slatted top of his desk. 'Good morning, Mr Holmes,' said Mrs Hudson's voice outside the door. 'I thought I heard you and the Doctor.'

'Good morning, Mrs Hudson,' he cried, opening the door. 'Yes, Watson and I are quite ready for breakfast now.'

Chapter Eleven

Wan Fat's Emporium

I had come down the stairs with my appetite sharpened by the chilly morning, but our encounter with the snake had all but extinguished my desire for food. Holmes, on the other hand, was full of cheer and bright conversation, as though the infiltration of a poisonous reptile into our sitting room was a good omen of some kind.

'Upon my word, Holmes,' I said, chuckling somewhat nervously in an attempt to match his lightness of mood, 'that episode before breakfast reminded rather of the affair at Stoke Moran.* Ten years ago, was it?'

'About that,' he agreed, 'but the snake had the advantage there.'

'How so?' I enquired.

'Because it was blind, and therefore equipped by nature with a superior sense of smell and an enhanced ability to detect heat and movement, whereas we – poorly provided creatures of the day – had to meet the infernal beast in the dark.'

'Nevertheless,' I said, you mastered the brute, as you dealt with its cousin this morning. I must say I am glad

---

* See *The Speckled Band* by Sir Arthur Conan Doyle.

your hand and eye have lost none of their cunning or strength.'

He smiled, as he always did when sincerely praised. 'Merely the result of long hours in the fencing salon of Maître Bencin as a boy. Fencing not only strengthens the wrist, but teaches a precise co-ordination of hand and eye. Be so good as to pass the toast.'

'Where do you think it came from?' I asked as I complied. 'This morning's visitor, I mean.'

'Where else but from our nocturnal burglar, Watson, which serves to confirm my speculations as to his identity.'

'But where would he have come by it?'

'As to that – unless our burglar breeds his own rattlesnakes, there is only one place that I know of in London where he might have obtained one. Do not dawdle about your tea, Watson. We have a visit to pay this morning.'

Not much more than an hour later we were in Chinatown, dropping from our hansom outside a large shop. Its windows were filled with cages in which small monkeys, rodents of various kinds and little cat-like creatures could be seen, while round its door hung more cages containing parrots, cockatoos, parakeets and mynahs, their gaudy feathers bright in the morning sun and their strange chattering delighting a bunch of ragged small boys who stood around the door. Over the entrance a sign, painted in gold on red, announced 'Wan Fat's Bird and Animal Emporium. Exotic Pets at Lowest Prices. Veterinary and Taxidermy Services'.

Inside, the shop was large, but low-ceilinged and dark after the sunlit street. Cages, tanks of plate glass and wooden hutches were piled about the walls in profusion, one upon another as high as a pile could be built, and their contents ranged from the domestic rabbit to lizards at whose origins I could not even guess. A musty smell, a compound of feathers and fur, animal droppings and feedstuffs, pervaded the whole place and wherever I looked eyes peered at me from between bars or from the shadow of hutches. There was a constant sound of scratching, twittering and whistling.

Something stirred in the darkest corner of the shop and a small, rotund Chinaman came forward to meet us. He was almost completely bald and his face was deeply wrinkled, while long whiskers drooped at each side of his mouth. He wore a magnificent silk gown, decorated with dragons and chrysanthemums, and his eyes twinkled from behind half-moon spectacles. 'Mr Holmes,' he greeted us, bowing slightly, then flinging his arms wide. 'How very good to see you. Too long altogether since you visit my humble emporium.'

'Wan Fat,' Holmes acknowledged, 'this is my colleague, Dr Watson.' His eyes roamed around the shop. 'I see that you continue to extend your stock.'

'Sailors, Mr Holmes, they bring these creatures from all over the world. They know they can sell to Wan Fat in London. Always I give best prices, sell at lowest prices. What for you come today, Mr Holmes? You like nice parrot, a mynah, talk to you, say what you want?'

'I thank you, Wan Fat, but I believe Baker Street can do without a parrot or a mynah,' Holmes said. 'I have come to ask you about this.' He opened the small Gladstone bag that he carried, drew out the dead snake and draped its length along Wan Fat's counter. It was the first time I had been able to take a leisurely view of the thing and I was surprised to note that it was nearly five feet long.

The little Chinaman's eyes opened wide. 'That was Percy,' he said. 'Where you find him?'

'In my sitting room coal scuttle,' Holmes answered. 'But I gather you knew the beast?'

'I had him here six, seven month. Bought him from American sailor. He kept him in box.'

'An American sailor?' said Holmes. 'Do you remember him?'

'He was big, tall, thin man, like you, Mr Holmes. Had red beard and earrings. Flying fish tattoos on both arms.'

'Not Danziger,' I remarked.

'No, indeed,' Holmes agreed. 'Tell me, Wan Fat, when did you buy Percy?'

The Chinese shopkeeper cast his eyes upwards. 'Six – seven month ago. My little grandson, he like him. He call him Percy, for boy at school.'

'And where do you think our friend Percy might have come from?' asked Holmes.

'He will be from America, Mr Holmes. Percy is diamond-back rattlesnake.'

'And whereabouts in America?' persisted Holmes.

'From west and south-west,' Wan Fat replied. 'Texas, New Mexico, California, Arizona.'

'And they are, of course, poisonous?'

The Chinaman's smiling face turned solemn. 'Very, very bad poison, Mr Holmes. Americans have sixty rattlesnakes, maybe more. Not all bad poison, but diamond-back he is very bad news.'

'And when did you sell him?'

'Two, three days ago. To man on docks.'

'What sort of man?' asked Holmes.

'He is foreign man. Brown skin. Not very tall. Hair black, eyes black.' He gestured with both hands at the sides of his head. 'Hair hang down side, like this. Wears band round head. I told him Percy very, very bad poison, but he say he no care. He know about snakes. Says he want snake to play joke on somebody.'

'So he did,' said Holmes, 'so he did. Why do you say this man works on the docks?'

'I see him three, four times look in shop window

when he coming from East India Dock. Think he work there, Mr Holmes.'

'Thank you, Wan Fat. Perhaps I could have a bag of birdseed for Mrs Hudson's budgerigar? And there is one more favour you might do me?'

'Anything, Mr Holmes. Anything at all,' said the shopkeeper, taking a fistful of seed from a large can and swiftly wrapping it in coloured paper.

Holmes pointed to the dead snake laid along the counter. 'Will you do me a kindness, Wan Fat?'

'You want me stuff him for you, Mr Holmes?'

My friend smiled and shook his head. 'I think not,' he said. 'Mrs Hudson is a woman of remarkable nerve, but I feel that a stuffed rattlesnake as an ornament in her lodgers' sitting room might prove just too much for her. No – I was thinking rather that you might be good enough to turn our friend here into a cigar case for me.'

The Chinaman smiled broadly. 'Will do, Mr Holmes. You want the meat? Rattlesnake very tasty. Fry up with ginger, water chestnut, little onions?'

'Thank you, no,' said Holmes. 'You may keep the meat, Wan Fat. I shall be quite satisfied with my cigar case.'

He paid for Mrs Hudson's birdseed and we left the shop.

'A cigar case!' I exclaimed.

'Why not, Watson? Why not? You know my liking for souvenirs of interesting cases. It seems to me that a cigar case made from the late Percy will form a fine conversation piece in years to come. Besides, he has materially assisted our enquiries.'

'Really?'

'Sometimes I fear that your memory is failing, Watson, though I believe it is merely a failure to note the repetition of themes and ideas.'

'What has been repeated?' I asked.

'Danziger the sailor and gunman came from Arizona. Our diamond-backed rattlesnake may also have come from that part of the United States. I am more certain than ever that I sent my wire to the right address.'

'How on earth does anyone manage to handle a poisonous reptile like that?' I wondered.

'There are people who have the skill,' said Holmes. 'The Moqui Indians of Arizona use live rattlesnakes in their ceremonies, putting the snake's head in their mouths, and there is a strange branch of the Baptist Church in America which handles them at their services.' He paused and looked about him. 'While we are in this district, Watson, do you fancy a little Chinese food?'

Thinking of rattlesnake fried with ginger, I refused his offer politely.

Chapter Twelve

Ominous Indications

There was no reply to Holmes's telegram waiting for us at Baker Street, but one arrived as we took our tea. Holmes read it over, then passed it across to me. 'It occurred to me', he explained, 'that if Teddy Danziger was a gunman from Arizona he would certainly be known in Tombstone, which is, apart from its unsavoury reputation for violence and corruption, the seat of the sheriff of Cochise County. Accordingly, I wired that official a description of Danziger, requesting any available information. So far from clearing the waters, I seem to have made them more cloudy. Here is his reply.'

The message read:

COUNTY SHERIFF'S OFFICE COCHISE COUNTY TOMBSTONE TERRITORY OF ARIZONA YOUR DESCRIPTION NOT OF ANYONE KNOWN TO THIS OFFICE OR TO OTHER LEGAL AGENCIES IN THIS TERRITORY STOP NAME OF EDMUND TEDDY DANZIGER ALSO NOT KNOWN AS GUNSLINGER BUT YOUR DESCRIPTION FITS WANTED MAN KNOWN AS INDIAN TOMMY SURNAME NOT KNOWN FORMER COWHAND WITH EDMUND DANZIGER CATTLEMAN AND BUSINESSMAN AT PHOENIX THIS TERRITORY STOP COPY OF YOUR WIRE FORWARDED TO DANZIGER FOR HIM TO REPLY SEPARATELY STOP WARRANTS HELD HERE

AGAINST INDIAN TOMMY INCLUDE MURDER STOP PLEASE
NOTIFY WHEREABOUTS THIS OFFICE STOP J SLAUGHTER SHER-
IFF COCHISE COUNTY

'Well,' I said when I had read it, 'so Danziger is not
really Danziger, but seems to have taken the name of his
former employer and is a gunman wanted for murder in
Arizona Territory. What do you make of it, Holmes?'

'Very little more than that,' he said, 'though it confirms my deductions about the so-called Teddy Danziger and strengthens the Arizona connection. I imagine
we shall have to wait until we hear from the real
Danziger.'

We had not long to wait. It was not much above half
an hour before another telegraph boy brought Danziger's message. It said:

PHOENIX ARIZONA TERRITORY WRITER HAS NEVER SET FOOT
IN ENGLAND AND CRIPPLING INJURY PREVENTS HIM SAILING
EVEN A HORSE THESE DAYS STOP PERSON DESCRIBED IN YOUR
WIRE CERTAINLY NOT ME BUT MAY BE INDIAN TOMMY SUR-
NAME UNKNOWN WHO WORKED FOR ME ON HAY RANCH AT
TULARE COUNTY CALIFORNIA MANY YEARS BACK STOP HE
WAS THEN ABOUT AGE SIXTEEN STOP HAD BEEN RAISED BY
INDIANS COMANCHES MESCALERO APACHES AND ARIZONA
APACHES TO AGE THIRTEEN STOP LEFT MY EMPLOY TO
BECOME COWBOY AND GUNSLINGER KNOWN TO TOMBSTONE
AUTHORITIES AND NOW WANTED FOR MURDER THERE STOP
WILL NOT COMMIT TO PUBLIC TELEGRAPH INFORMATION
INDIAN TOMMY GAVE ME THEN BUT REFER YOU TO MY OLD
FRIEND MAJOR JOHN T BRAITHWAITE US CAVALRY RETIRED
STOP HE ARRIVES GORDONS HOTEL LONDON SATURDAY ON
BUSINESS AND HAS MY PERMISSION TO TELL YOU WHATEVER
YOU NEED TO KNOW STOP ASK HIM ABOUT PERALTA STOP
GOOD HUNTING STOP EDMUND F DANZIGER

'A white man raised by Indians!' I exclaimed. 'You have
certainly stirred the right pot, Holmes. Here is your

Apache Indian connection and who knows what more.'

'My wire has yielded better results than I expected,' he said. 'Not least the prospect of learning who, where or what peralta may be. Now, I must drop a line to Major Braithwaite at Gordon's, to await his arrival.'

'What will you do until Danziger's friend arrives?' I asked.

'Wan Fat's information and the unforthcoming nature of Mr Graby both suggest to me that I might profitably spend a little time around the docks. I shall organise a suitable disguise tomorrow and see if I cannot discover both our burglar and what it is that Graby concealed from us.'

'You are sure that he did not tell us the truth?'

'Positive,' he replied. 'It is in the eyes, Watson. The repeated downward and leftward flicker of the eyes is a reflex that only the most hardened liar can control. Graby told us as much of the truth as he wished. There is more and I shall discover it.'

In the event, my friend's plans were forestalled by a third message.

We were breaking our fast the next morning when Mrs Hudson brought yet another telegram to our table. This time I could see that it was of the inland variety.

'Hah!' exclaimed Holmes when he had opened it. 'Look at this, Watson! Captain Napley has done well for us.'

The message was from Portmadoc and said:

MISSING VESSEL MOORED HERE IN GOOD ORDER STOP NO SIGN OF THE AMERICAN BUT OMINOUS INDICATIONS

'Where is Portmadoc?' I asked. 'It is in Ulster, is it not? What would Danziger and *Gyrfalcon* be doing there?'

Holmes snorted. 'Watson! In the first place he is not Danziger, as we now know – he is Indian Tommy – and in the second place Portmadoc is not in Ulster but in north Wales. It is the port from which it is erroneously believed that Prince Madoc ap Llewellyn sailed to discover America in the twelfth century.'

'You mean that he did not discover America?'

'No,' he snapped. 'I mean than he did not sail from Portmadoc. The name has other and more recent connotations. Finish your breakfast, Watson. We must join Napley as soon as we may and see what he means by "ominous indications". Be so good as to ring for our boots.'

Holmes's temper improved after we had settled into a railway carriage. Once he brought his mind to bear on a problem he applied virtually all his energy until the matter was solved. Delays and dead ends were enormously frustrating to him, and his mind would race uselessly in the absence of data, making him irritable and an uncertain companion. The tide of information that had flowed in with the three telegrams had pleased him greatly and throughout our long journey to north Wales he discoursed amusingly on the Welsh discovery of America, the practice of tattooing among French criminals, rhyming cant and the proper techniques of knife-throwing, among many other subjects.

It was early evening when we finally arrived at the little Welsh port and Captain Napley was at our lodgings to meet us.

'You have done well, Captain, to locate *Gyrfalcon* so swiftly,' said Holmes, shaking the seaman's hand.

'Nothing much, as it turned out, sir. A few shillings on telegrams to a few friends here and there, and I heard as she was up this way.'

'Have you been aboard her?' asked Holmes.

Napley nodded. 'I have, sir, but only briefly. When I saw her, I had to row out and make sure as she was all right, which I did, but that was when I saw what I called "ominous indications" in my wire, sir. I thought it best as you should see exactly how the land lay, so I left her as she was. It's my opinion that foul play has taken place on *Gyrfalcon*.'

Holmes glanced at the sun and pulled out his watch. 'Then we had better forgo our refreshments for the time being, Watson, and let Captain Napley show us *Gyrfalcon* while the light holds. Is she far, Captain?'

'No, sir. Not at all. Just a short pull out into the harbour.'

He took us down the quayside, alongside little fishing boats and battered coastal schooners, pausing at one point to indicate where our quarry lay out in the harbour, rocking gently on a slight swell, her main mast swaying like a slow pendulum. She was a smart vessel and I could well believe her racing reputation, but her distinctive dark-red paintwork was marred by the long scrape on her port side that Mr Morris had mentioned to us.

We were rapidly alongside her and scrambling aboard. As soon as we stood on her deck, Holmes put out a hand to warn the captain and me not to move. It was easy to see why. The clean planking of *Gyrfalcon*'s deck and the roof of her cabin were splashed here and there with what appeared to be dried blood.

Holmes stood still, bracing himself against the slight motion of the vessel, while his keen eyes swivelled about. 'Do you know how long she has been here?' he asked Napley at length.

'From the harbour master's records, sir, it seems as Danziger brought her here straight from Eacham, about the time as Mr Crosby vanished.'

'That can only have been to conceal either *Gyrfalcon* or the American or both,' said my friend. 'Has the American been seen here lately?'

Captain Napley shook his head. 'No, sir. He brought her in single-handed and told the harbour master as he expected to be here a little while, awaiting orders from his owner. He stayed on board her for a few days, then he went and her dinghy was tied up at the quayside. The harbour master just thought he'd had orders to go ashore and would be back in due course.'

Holmes looked around him. 'I very much doubt that he will be back,' he observed and began to pace about the deck, stooping to examine each of the bloodstains carefully.

After a while he straightened up and rejoined us. 'It is clear what has happened here,' he said. 'The American was standing there, beside the cabin, with his back to the quay, when he was strnck by an arrow in the back.'

'An arrow!' exclaimed Napley.

'The first or second of two,' Holmes stated. 'If you observe that mark across the curvature of the cabin roof, where the varnish is scratched, I think you will agree that either the first or second missile missed its mark and struck the cabin. The American, hit by whichever arrow, fell forward against the roof, bleeding copiously. I suspect that the arrow's head had passed right through, or he would not have bled at the front.' He pointed with his stick. 'There', he said, 'are the marks that show he was not killed instantly. You can see that he lay bleeding on the deck for a while, then pulled himself towards the cabin companionway.' He stepped towards the entrance to the yacht's cabin. 'He stumbled down into the cabin,' Holmes continued, and stepped down himself.

We followed him in. If the bloodstains on the deck had seemed ominous, the cabin looked like a shambles. Pools of blood had been spilled in the small space and great splashes of it had erupted in several places. Fittings were broken or awry and some of the floorboards had been taken up.

Holmes stooped and picked up a pistol from the floor. I could see at once that it was the pair of the one we had found in the American's lodgings.

'I was evidently wrong, Watson, when I said that he

took no weapon with him from London. He seems to have been one of those who use two pistols, though the wear from fanning on the hammer of this one shows that he used them independently, emptying one, then switching to the second.'

He took out his matches and lit the lantern that hung above us, then carefully scrutinised the cabin's walls. 'He never had occasion to fire the weapon,' he observed, after he had completed his examination. 'Not only are there no bullet holes anywhere, there was no smell of gunpowder when we entered.'

'Would there be, after such a long time?' I asked.

'Oh, yes,' he said. 'Weapons like this emit a very large blast of fumes and unburned powder when they are fired, and this cabin has been closed since the incident. No cap-and-ball weapon has been fired in here, so we may take it that his assailant was not injured.'

I looked around at the wrecked cabin. 'But the American seems to have fought fiercely, despite his wounds,' I remarked.

'Not so, Watson,' he replied. 'The American will have been dying when his assailant came aboard. Most of the disorder here comes from a search. You do not open drawers and cupboards in the course of a fight, nor take up floorboards, beside which, none of the bloodstaining is inside cupboards and drawers. They were opened after blood was shed.' He pointed to the gap in the boards. 'He will have wrenched those up to gain access to the ballast, I take it, Captain?'

'Yes indeed, sir,' said Napley, 'but what about all this blood if they never fought?'

'That', said Holmes, 'appears to be the result of the way in which the American died. It is mostly the product of a single great eruption of blood, no doubt occurring when the attacker removed the dead man's head. I think we shall have to warn the local police to seek two separate parts of Indian Tommy.'

Chapter Thirteen

An Evening With Lestrade

Further search of the vessel revealed that the American had, indeed, been alone aboard her before the attack. His murderer had, however, remained on *Gyrfalcon* for some time after killing and decapitating *Gyrfalcon*'s 'second captain', for Holmes drew our attention to the boat's little galley, where a tin of meat had been opened by someone with bloodstained hands and its contents consumed. A large tin of ships' biscuits had also been broached and sampled, but a tin of fish had been opened and its contents left to moulder uneaten.

'It appears', Holmes remarked, 'that the killer helped himself from the galley while carrying out a thorough search of *Gyrfalcon*. He is, however, a man of simple tastes – beef and biscuits he will eat, but fish does not appeal to him.'

I shuddered at the thought of a man who could create the carnage witnessed by the stains in the saloon and then satisfy his hunger on salt beef and hard tack.

'Come Watson, Captain,' said my friend. 'There is nothing more to learn here. In the morning I shall wire Lestrade to communicate with the local police and we shall return to London. You, Captain, may inform your employer of your success in finding a valuable asset for her.'

We made our way back in the dinghy, Holmes asking Napley to row us alongside the quay until he spotted the unmistakable streaks of *Gyrfalcon*'s dark-red paint on the timbers, showing us where she had come to minor grief against the pilings.

'Do you think that the attacker succeeded in finding what he sought?' I asked Holmes as we made our way from the quayside to our lodgings.

'How can we know, Watson? We have no idea what he sought, nor whether it was aboard *Gyrfalcon*. There is no way of knowing. We must wait and see what his next move may be.'

Holmes and I left Portmadoc early the next day, after Holmes had wired Lestrade and Mrs Crosby. Captain Napley refused to accompany us, saying that he would await Mrs Crosby's instructions in Portmadoc and keep an eye on *Gyrfalcon*.

From the far north-west of Wales to London is a long trip by rail and I was not sorry when our hansom drew up outside 221b Baker Street. I was looking forward to a good dinner and an early night, but it was not to be. As we entered our sitting room we found Inspector Lestrade awaiting us.

'Good evening Mr Holmes, Doctor,' he greeted us. 'You found *Gyrfalcon*, then?'

'I set in train events which led to her being found,' replied Holmes. 'You have evidently received my telegram.'

Lestrade nodded, looking pleased with himself. 'I have and I popped round to tell you that I have the answers to your questions, Mr Holmes.'

'What questions were those, Holmes?' I enquired.

'I wired Lestrade to tell him that *Gyrfalcon* was at Portmadoc, but I also asked him to warn the police in north Wales to look out for a headless corpse and suggested that Scotland Yard might receive another parcel. They were hardly questions, Lestrade.'

Lestrade's rat-like features twisted into a broad grin. 'Maybe not, Mr Holmes, but they raised questions, if I may say so.'

'And you say that you have the answers,' said Holmes, falling into an armchair and reaching in his pocket for his pipe. 'Then you had better take the basket chair and help yourself to a cheroot.'

The little detective reached for the coal scuttle where Holmes stored his cigars.

'By the way,' remarked Holmes, 'we found a rattlesnake among the cigars the other day.'

Lestrade's hand paused in midair. 'A rattlesnake, Mr Holmes? Are you pulling my leg? We don't get rattlesnakes in England!'

'Watson and I, it seems, get rattlesnakes in our sitting room. However, I believe the problem is ended and you may safely take a cheroot.'

Once his cheroot was well alight Lestrade said, 'I admit that I was surprised to hear from you in north Wales, Mr Holmes. It never crossed my mind that *Gyrfalcon* might be up there.'

'Which is precisely why Scotland Yard did not find her,' my friend explained. 'Once you knew that she was not in any of the obvious yachting harbours of England or the Continent, I should have thought that the next place to search was in Britain's less obvious harbours, as Captain Napley did when I instructed him. Now, what are these answers you have to the questions that I did not ask in my wire?'

'Ah,' said Lestrade, 'the first is the question of Danziger's head. That, I'm afraid, has turned up at Scotland Yard in a similar state to Crosby's, Mr Holmes. I did not bring it with me. I felt it was somehow, I don't know, indelicate perhaps, to be riding about in omnibuses with somebody's head in a box.'

'Your sensitivity does you credit, Lestrade,' agreed Holmes, with a perfectly straight face. 'Do I understand that the American's head had been shrunk in the same fashion as Crosby's?'

'Exactly, Mr Holmes. Now as to the remainder of Edmund Danziger, I should tell you that the police in Caernarvonshire found him on a beach some weeks past and, nobody having claimed him and there being no identification of him, have consigned him to a pauper's grave.'

'That is a pity,' mused Holmes, 'though a pauper's grave may be better than he would have merited in his own country. Are you sure it was the American, Lestrade? The Atlantic ships from the Mersey pass by north Wales and there is a considerable coastal traffic. It is not just some hapless fellow fallen from a passing vessel?'

Lestrade took his notebook from his pocket and thumbed through it. 'Their description', he said, 'was of a large man, with fair hair about his body, and they most particularly noted a curious pattern that seemed to have been cut all over his back with a knifepoint, though their surgeon was of the view that it was a very old injury. Their surgeon also thought that the man was between thirty and forty years old and that his head had been removed with a single blow of an axe.' He closed the book.

'Was the axe blow inflicted by a left-handed man?' asked Holmes.

Lestrade looked at him with surprise. 'They did not say, Mr Holmes. I suppose their doctor had no views on the point.'

'Another pity,' said Holmes. Still, unless a better candidate turns up, I think we may reasonably accept that the remains were those of the American. Incidentally,

Lestrade, his name was not Danziger; that was an alias.'

'Really? What was his proper name then, Mr Holmes?'

'So far as I can at present determine, he was best known as "Indian Tommy". You should inform the sheriff of Cochise County in the Arizona Territory of the death. He has an outstanding warrant for murder against the late Indian Tommy.'

'The sheriff of where? A warrant for murder?' exclaimed the detective. 'Oh, now, Mr Holmes, you are certainly pulling my leg!'

'Not at all, and if Watson will be good enough to ring for Mrs Hudson, I shall invite you to dine with us so that I may bring you up to date on the enquiries which Watson and I have been pursuing.'

Over dinner, Holmes was as good as his word, detailing our every move from our call at Graby's chandlery, our visit to Mrs Crosby, our investigations at Eacham with their attendant alarm, our sinister visitor and our journey to north Wales. He showed the little detective the telegrams from Arizona and the strange document which Mrs Crosby had handed to us. By the end of his recital Lestrade's head shook slowly and continuously in wonder.

When the meal was over we lit cigars and pipes. 'I have to say, Mr Holmes, that what you have told me beats everything I have ever heard,' said Lestrade. 'But what does it all mean?'

'The meaning of some of it is simple and obvious,' Holmes answered. 'Beginning from the beginning – Crosby was a man with a sporting temperament, but whose finances were considerably overstretched. You have heard how he tried to remedy that condition by joining Knight's treasure hunt on Trinidad Island. The application of whatever financial skills he possessed does not seem to have appealed to him as a way out of his problems; rather he looked for something more adventurous – a decision fully in keeping with the kind of man he seems to have been.'

'You think that he did find a treasure, then?' enquired Lestrade.

'I doubt very much that he succeeded where Knight's party failed, if that is what you imply. On the other hand, during his last transatlantic voyage he seems to have become involved in a scheme which could have been designed to appeal to him, inasmuch as it embodied risk and a great profit if it was successful. Whether that scheme was broached to him in the United States, or more probably in Demerara, I know not, but it is certain that the American Indian Tommy was deeply involved.'

'And what was that scheme, Mr Holmes?' asked Lestrade.

'It was to bring something of great value to England aboard *Gyrfalcon* in secrecy. Now, the requirement of secrecy was such that Crosby would not have his captain or his crew know what was going forward and went to elaborate lengths to keep them from finding out, both when the cargo was loaded in Demerara and when it was offloaded in England, or more probably in Wales.'

'And what do you think it was, Mr Holmes?'

'I believe that it was either treasure in the sense that it is commonly meant – valuable plate, jewels and so on – or precious metal in bulk. I now tend to the latter view, since there are still gold mines in north Wales, not so very far from where Crosby and the American brought their cargo ashore. If they had shipped gold or silver in some crude form, it would be possible to have it reduced to an unrecognisable and more marketable form in that area, and Crosby had the contacts to turn the metal into cash.'

'I see,' Lestrade nodded. 'That makes sense of all that

fiddling about with the ballast and it explains why Mrs Crosby is better off than she might have expected to be, but I don't see where killing people and shrinking their heads comes into it.'

'If Knight had returned from Trinidad Island with the treasure of Lima,' said Holmes, 'he would not have been stopped from landing it in England and disposing of it as he wished. The same applies to Crosby; he might have sailed into any British port with heaps of gold and silver upon his decks and no one would have said him nay, but he did not do so. Instead he took elaborate precautions against even his crew knowing what was aboard *Gyrfalcon*.'

'But why, Mr Holmes?' Lestrade wanted to know, like an impatient child being told a story.

'Because what they shipped was illegally acquired, I imagine; because someone else had a claim on it and would seek to prevent its shipment to England. Furthermore, whoever that may be, having failed to prevent the treasure reaching England, set out to prevent Crosby and Indian Tommy from enjoying the fruits of their crime by tracking them down and killing them.'

'But why by torturing them and cutting off their heads?' asked the Inspector.

'There', said Holmes, 'we come to the question of who it is that has carried out these killings.'

'You know who?' exclaimed Lestrade.

'Hold hard, Lestrade. I did not say so. However, I do know a certain amount about your murderer. I do not yet know if he is the wronged party, or merely his or her agent, but I do know what manner of man we are looking for – an American redskin of the Apache tribe.'

'An Apache!' exclaimed Lestrade. 'Surely not, Mr Holmes!'

'On the contrary,' said Holmes, 'the arrow fired at me in Hampshire made clear a proposition that I was already considering. Such descriptions as we have had of the man – from Graby and from Wan Fat – only confirm it. Wan Fat was even good enough to suggest where the man works when he is in London: the East India Dock.'

'Sure enough!' said the Scotland Yard man. 'Then all we need to do is watch the dock and feel his collar when he turns up.'

'Oh, by all means,' Holmes agreed. 'But when you have caught your man, what sort of a case against him have you? You have not one witness who can speak of an illegal act committed by him. You have no single piece of evidence that can be carried home to him. How will you prove torture and murder against him, Lestrade, let alone the business with the heads, which is probably an offence against the Blasphemy Act?'

'I don't know,' admitted Lestrade, crestfallen.

'Then I suggest you keep your men away from the docks and leave him to me for a little while.'

Chapter Fourteen

A Shavetail Goes West

For two days afterwards I saw Holmes only at breakfast, after which he would return to his room and emerge, heavily disguised, to make his way to the docks. At what hour he returned home I do not know.

Sunday came and Holmes desisted from his efforts in the East End. Despite his long days and nights he was up early, ate a hearty breakfast and passed the morning in sardonic comments on the Sunday newspapers. I took his affable mood to be confirmation that his enquiries about the docks were proceeding well.

We were both sprawled in a post-prandial torpor brought on by Mrs Hudson's Sunday luncheon when our landlady showed in a liveried messenger boy from Gordon's Hotel. He had brought Holmes a note and awaited a reply.

'Are you engaged tomorrow evening, Watson?' asked Holmes. 'We are invited to dine.'

He passed me the note and I saw that it was a sheet of quarto bond, embossed with the hotel's address. The text read:

Dear Mr Holmes,

Teddy Danziger in Tucson has wired me that I could expect to hear from you and your note waited for me on my arrival yesterday. Teddy also says that I should assist you in any way I can.

As I know no one in London, you would be doing me a great kindness if you would agree to dine here with me at eight on Monday. At the same time we can see how I can help you and if I can I will.

Yours faithfully,

John T. Braithwaite,

 Major, Third US Cavalry, Retired

I confirmed that I had no appointment that would prevent me joining Holmes and the Major, and Holmes scribbled a quick acceptance.

The Major was waiting for us in the smoking room at Gordon's on Monday evening and rose to welcome us. He was a tall, lean man, though broad at the shoulder, and seemed about fifty. His close-cut hair was pure silver, above a long, weathered face, which displayed blue eyes, a pendulous nose and a wide mouth. His light coat was open, displaying a richly decorative waistcoat.

When the hotel's boy had announced us our host introduced himself – 'Major James T. Braithwaite, Third United States Cavalry, Retired' – and shook us both warmly by the hand.

'And', said Holmes, 'I suspect, a native of Boston and a graduate of the University of Harvard.'

Braithwaite's jaw dropped. 'Now how in blazes do you know that? You certainly never read it in my long Yankee looks.'

'No, Major, but your accent, though altered by many years in the West, is Bostonian and you wear a Harvard fraternity ring.'

Braithwaite laughed. 'I was about to remark', he said,

'that I have followed your exploits in print and I am honoured to meet you both. I was delighted to hear from Danziger that you were alive and well, Mr Holmes.'

'No doubt Watson will give the world a highly embellished account of my return at some point, Major, but for the moment let me say that I have never been quite so easy to kill as my opponents have believed.'

Our host laughed again and waved us to armchairs while he ordered drinks.

'Are you long out of the Army?' Holmes asked when our drinks had arrived.

'No, sir. I wore the blue coat for twenty-five years, almost all of it in the West, and I wouldn't have traded it for any other profession, but a man's bones get older and he begins to hanker for a feather bed at night, not a blanket in the desert or a barrack room bunk. So, here I am in London, as a sort of commission agent for Teddy Danziger and others. The Arizona Territory is a place which has great possibilities and we aim to make it known to the world.'

'That was where you served?' asked Holmes.

Braithwaite nodded. 'Most of my time was in Arizona,' he said. 'I went there just after the war as a bright young shavetail lieutenant. I'd missed the war by the time I joined up and I didn't want to hang about some eastern post, and the only place there was any fighting going on was out West, so I went.'

I had not heard the word 'shavetail' before, but its connotation was evident. 'It's a hard country, I believe,' I remarked.

'It's been said that Arizona is both heaven and hell,' he said. 'It's one of the most beautiful places in the world and one of the most frightening. Add to that the fact that it's got just about every kind of weather you ever heard of. The same patrol would take you through desert at one hundred and twenty degrees and in hours you'd be in the mountains in deep snow. Where I was posted first – at old Camp Grant – they used to tell about the soldier who died and went to hell. Three nights after he died the sentries saw his ghost prowling the post and asked him what he was about. Well, they say that he said he'd come back to fetch his blankets because hell was too cold for him after Camp Grant.'

We chuckled and Holmes said, 'And you had the Apaches as well, Major.'

'The Apaches?' Braithwaite repeated. 'So we did. We had the Apaches. Now there's a breed of men who know how to live in that country. Desert or mountain, it's all the same to them.'

'You admire them?' asked Holmes.

'Indeed I do, Mr Holmes. When I went West I sub-scribed to the old belief that the only good Indian is a dead Indian, but I soon saw the other side of it. We have a Constitution that says that "all men are created equal" and we fought the war to make black folks free, but we took the Indians' land from them, refused them a vote and wouldn't even give them the right to be heard in the courts.' He shook his head sadly and at that moment a waiter summoned us to the dining toom.

Once we were settled and our orders placed our host filled our glasses and began again: 'You were asking about the Apaches. That isn't their true name, you know. Apache is a name that the Spanish picked up from other Indians in the old days. They call themselves "Tinneh", which means "people', but "Apache" means "enemy" and that just about says it all. They are as professional an enemy as any army could wish to meet. They can run for ever without tiring, live on nothing, climb like cats and put an arrow into anything that moves at about any range.'

Holmes grimaced slightly and Braithwaite continued: 'They fought the Spaniards like wildcats back in the old days and they gave us a lot of trouble when we first moved in. But we had them settled down, largely, after a while. Even their chief Cochise was contracting to cut firewood for the stage company and if they went raiding it tended to be into Mexico. Then that goddarned fool Bascom stirred it all up.'

'What did he do?' I asked.

'Well, a kid called Micky Free – half-Irish and half-Mexican – was taken by the Indians, and Bascom asked Cochise to come and talk to him about it. Cochise, he thought he was going to be asked to set up a deal to get the boy back, because it wasn't his people who had the boy, but Bascom accused Cochise of taking the boy, and tried to arrest him and his brother. Cochise got away, but his brother was killed. After that Cochise forgot about Mexicans and went after Americans.'

He took a long drink. 'Thanks to Bascom,' he went on, 'we had hell to pay with Cochise for years. Then the government made General Crook the Commandant of Arizona Territory. Now, Crook was a man who knew how to deal with Indians. If they wanted fighting, he knew how to fight them, but when he talked to them they knew he always spoke the truth, so in the end he got them settled down again.'

He lifted his glass in a toast. 'George Crook', he said, 'was the finest man I ever knew, God rest him. When he'd put Arizona Territory to rights, they sent him up north and I was deeply honoured that he took me on his staff when he was up on the Rosebud campaign.'

'The Rosebud campaign?' I asked. 'You served alongside General Custer?'

'So I did,' he replied, 'and I reckon it's a shame that you recognise Custer's name but not Crook's. Custer was nothing but a bag of wind, a glory hunter who mistreated his men and saw the Indian campaigns as a road to fame. If Custer had stuck to his orders he'd be alive now and so would his men.'

'What happened to the boy – Micky Free?' I enquired.

He grinned. 'Micky Free grew up to be a cavalry scout and, having regard to the kind or ornery character he became, I can't say that the war with Cochise was worth it.'

'You were telling us', said Holmes, 'how the Apaches fight.'

'Hit and run away,' Braithwaite explained. 'They knew every cave and hideout in the mountains. They'd hit a ranch and then run for the mountains. They travelled light – far lighter than we did with equipment and ammunition on mule trains – and they'd disappear and we'd have to go hunting them for days and weeks. They'd make sneak attacks, even right into our posts. They'd creep in under cover of darkness and put an arrow into a sentry or anyone who was unlucky enough to walk in their sight, then they'd melt away before we even knew anything had happened. They're expert at covering their tracks. They'll travel miles with their feet wrapped in bags of grass to hide their tracks. They can run like nobody else in the world and they'll eat anything that lives – excepting fish.'

I recalled the can of mouldering fish in *Gyrfalcon*'s galley and the strange imprints at the American's lodgings and in our sitting room. Despite the evidence of the arrow in Hampshire, I had not been entirely convinced by Holmes's theorising, but Braithwaite's confirmations reminded me of my friend's long-standing objection to coincidence as an explanation of events.

'So, in sum,' said Holmes, 'you believe that the Apache is fierce, clever and resourceful, a warrior who knows when to fight and when to run, a stalker and killer by stealth, athletic and a fine archer.'

Braithwaite nodded. 'That about puts it in a nutshell.'

'Do they take the heads of their victims?' asked Holmes.

'They do, Mr Holmes. I've seen as many as seven heads on the parade ground when we've sent out loyal Apaches to bring renegades in. They used to bring the heads in to prove to us that they'd killed the right men.'

I was moved by an impulse of disgust until I recollected that I had known white police officers in Australia to remove the heads of dead men for identification purposes.

Holmes seemed to think for a moment. 'Do they', he asked at last, 'follow the practice of the Jivaros of South America and certain Far Eastern tribes and shrink the heads of their enemies?'

'I can't say that I have ever seen such,' said our host, 'but I've heard it suggested. Like all the Indians they keep sacred places where they hide objects that they believe are powerful magic and I've heard tell that some of the things they keep are the heads of their enemies – not the skulls, but the heads. I guess they might shrink them for that purpose.'

At this gruesome point in our conversation our meals were served and talk languished until the waiters had gone. For a few minutes after being served we ate in silence, then Braithwaite asked, 'May I enquire what is your interest in Apaches, Mr Holmes? They seem to be rather far from London to be of relevance.'

'My interest', Holmes replied, 'arises because two men have been brutally murdered, one here in London and one in north Wales. All the indications point to an Apache Indian as the perpetrator of these crimes. A number of things which you have said tonight have only served to confirm my own deductions.'

Braithwaite stared at Holmes. 'An Apache!' he exclaimed. 'Killing people? Here in London? Isn't that pretty unlikely?'

'Oh, I agree with you entirely, Major, but it is an odd and well-tried maxim of mine that once you have assembled the facts and defined the impossible, whatever remains, however improbable, must be the truth. Now, however improbable it may seem to you, I believe that an Apache has killed two men in Britain and, were it not for the alertness of Watson here, I might well have joined them. May I tell you about it?'

'You surely may, Mr Holmes. I'm all ears.'

Chapter Fifteen

The Peralta Legend

As we ate Holmes outlined succinctly the sequence of events from Lestrade's first appearance at Baker Street with his grim parcel, adding his own deductions as he went. Braithwaite listened in fascination, only occasionally asking a question. When Holmes had finished the Major sat, shaking his head slowly in amazement. 'That', he said at last, 'is the most peculiar story I have ever heard, Mr Holmes. If you will permit me to pass it on at home, I reckon I can dine out for the rest of my life on that tale.'

Holmes smiled. 'Why not, Major, but my tale has no ending, and that is why I trespass upon your hospitality.'

'Anything I can do, Mr Holmes, I shall. I told you from the first that Teddy Danziger gave me carte blanche to tell you whatever you wished to know.'

'Your friend Danziger seems to believe that this affair has something to do with something or someone he calls "peralta",' said Holmes. 'Perhaps if we were to return to the smoking room you would be kind enough to explain to us what he meant.'

As we made our way to the hotel's smoking room I reflected that the only thing Holmes had omitted from his account of the affair had been any mention of the document which Mrs Crosby had given him.

Once we were seated and had cigars well alight, Braithwaite began his narrative. 'Peralta', he said, 'was a person and may also be a place. It may be just a piece of nonsense, but I've heard enough about it through the years to believe that there's truth at the back of it.' He paused and drew on his cigar. 'I reckon the story really began back when the old Spaniards owned Mexico and New Mexico and Arizona, but I don't think I need to go that far back. Let me just go back about a quarter century – to seventy-one. There was a man in Arizona then called Dr Walker. He was a medical doctor and they say he was partly of Indian blood. He'd also been a soldier; in fact he commanded the Pima Maricopa Company.'

'Those are Indian names,' observed Holmes.

'Correct,' said the Major. 'The Company was formed of loyal Indians from those two tribes and Dr Walker led them against the Apaches. Now the doctor seems to have had a bit of General Crook in him, because he fought the Apaches successfully, but he also cared about what happened to the Indians and he stayed among them, particularly with the Pimas.'

He sucked on his cigar again. 'It was while he was doctoring with the Pimas, about seventy-one, that two Pimas brought a sick white man to him. Well, it didn't take much to see that this man had been shot in the shoulder with an arrow and the wound had become infected. He was in a pretty bad state, but Walker cleaned him up and patched him up and hoped for the best.'

The Major took a long draught from his port. 'Now this fellow that the Pimas brought in said he was from Germany – a Dutchman, as we called them – and he and a partner had fought for the Confederacy in the war.

108

When the war was over, like a lot more Confederate soldiers, they drifted West and at some point they were in Mexico. While they were there, they stepped into some kind of brawl and saved the life of a man called Don Miguel Peralta. So there's Peralta the person.'

'And what manner of person was Don Miguel Peralta?' asked Holmes.

'He was a Mexican, of the old Spanish blood, and he owned a big spread down there. Now, he was mighty grateful to the Dutchman and his partner – by the way, the Dutchman's name was Jacob Weiser – for saving his hide and he offered them a deal by way of a reward. He explained to them', Braithwaite continued, 'that his family owned a rich gold deposit in Arizona Territory. His father had been killed there, by the Apaches, and Don Miguel wanted to make an expedition there, but he reckoned he needed fighting men, so he offered Weiser and his partner one half of any gold they took out.'

'From Mexico – even the border – into Arizona is a long journey,' observed Holmes. 'He must have had great faith in his mine.'

'Oh, he did,' said our host, 'he did. As Weiser told it to Doc Walker, they made it to the mine, with a party of Don Miguel's peons, all heavily armed, and they succeeded in taking gold worth sixty thousand dollars back to Mexico.'

'Sixty thousand dollars!' I exclaimed. 'That's a stupendous sum!'

'So it is, Doctor, but that's the figure and I had this tale from someone who heard it from Doc Walker himself.'

'And, no doubt, Weiser and his partner went back,' said Holmes.

Braithwaite raised a hand. 'Hold hard, Mr Holmes. That isn't quite the way of it. Once they had the gold back in Mexico, Don Miguel offered Weiser and his partner another deal. He said that he was getting old and he had no kin. If they would let him have most of their share of the gold, he would make over the mine to them.'

'Which they accepted?' asked Holmes.

'They did, indeed. Don Miguel Peralta gave them a signed deed to the mine and a map – supposedly on a piece of rawhide – showing them how to find it again.'

'Weiser seems to have told a long story, for a man who was seriously injured,' Holmes remarked.

Braithwaite smiled. 'The way I heard it, Weiser lived for about three days or more under the Doctor's care, but on the second day he developed pneumonia. When he knew that he wasn't going to make it, he told his whole story to Doc Walker. He said that they had gone back to the mine and worked it till their supplies were running low. Then his partner set out to fetch supplies, saying that he'd be back on the fourth day, but he didn't come back. On the fifth day the Apaches jumped Weiser and he only just escaped, but with an arrow in his shoulder. Somehow he managed to make it across the desert to a Pima village and they took him to Doc Walker. Well, he reckoned the Apaches had got his friend and he was a dying man, so he gave Doc Walker the map and told him the mine was his. Then he died.'

Braithwaite paused and gazed into his glass before taking another drink.

'What did the doctor do with the map?' asked Holmes.

'Well, now. Doc Walker was getting married that year – to a Pima girl – and he wasn't in a hurry to go back to the area where he'd whipped the Apaches at the battle of Apache Leap. He had a feeling they might remember him unkindly, so he didn't do anything with the map. The way it turned out, he never needed to because some time after, the Pimas showed him a silver mine called the Vekol mine. He got so rich from that, they say he's spent millions of dollars on the Pimas and the Maricopas.'

'So the story of the Peralta mine rests on the word of one wandering German who was a seriously sick man when he told it,' Holmes mused. 'What happened to Weiser's map?'

'That I don't know,' said Braithwaite. 'But what you should have asked me was what happened to Weiser's partner.'

'But the Apaches killed him,' I protested. 'You told us so.'

Braithwaite shook his head and Sherlock Holmes smiled. 'Not so, Watson,' he said. 'Major Braithwaite told us only that Weiser believed the Apaches had killed his partner, though it was a reasonable inference. What did happen to him, Major?'

'If you'll be good enough to push the bell for another drink, I'll be pleased to tell you,' said our host and once our glasses were replenished he began again: 'Jacob Weiser's partner was another Dutchman and another Jacob, called Jacob Waltz. They'd known each other since boys and their families had come over to the States together, way back before the war. Now, it seems that everything that Weiser told the doctor was true, because Waltz confirmed it later.'

'To whom?' demanded Holmes.

'Don't rush me, Mr Holmes. That'll come in a while.'

He took a drink. 'A few years after Weiser's death, Waltz fetched up in Phoenix. Where he'd been in between is anybody's guess, but they say that he lived with the Pimas for a time. He bought some land on the south side of the town, but he didn't stay there. It seems like he was restless – there's those who say he felt guilty over Weiser's death – and he wandered about a lot. Suffice it to say that he turned up back in Phoenix in the late eighties and built himself an adobe – that's a clay house – on his land. He grew alfalfa and he raised chickens, and he kept himself to himself. He got a reputation as some kind of hermit and folks said that he always seemed to look sad. They said afterwards that he looked that way because he believed he'd caused his partner's death, but then, they said all kinds of things about him, including that he murdered Weiser.'

Once more Braithwaite looked thoughtfully into his glass. Holmes took out his briar pipe and began to fill it. I was aching to ask the Major how Waltz had survived, but I forbore.

'Waltz used to deliver eggs to a near neighbour, a Mrs Helena Thomas, and she and her boy were the nearest to friends that Waltz had. She had been deserted by her husband, but she had a boy of about sixteen – not her own, so it seems, but a German boy whom the Thomases had adopted. After Charley Thomas disappeared, his wife set up a bakery business and a little soda fountain and ice cream parlour.'

'A soda fountain?' I queried.

'I guess you might say a place that sells soft drinks,' Braithwaite replied. 'Anyway, Mrs Thomas had no good head for business and allowed too much credit. By about five years ago she was deep in trouble, owing about twelve or thirteen hundred dollars and with no way to pay. One day she poured out her troubles to old Jacob Waltz. Well, she says that he was fond of her adopted boy because he could talk German with him, but whatever the reason, Waltz offered to help her out.'

'He had money from the mine?' I said.

'Hear me out, Doctor. Waltz swore Mrs Thomas and her boy to secrecy, then he produced about fifteen hundred dollars' worth of gold dust. He told her that she mustn't let on that she had all the money, but must pay her debts by instalments. He shipped the dust to Frisco and gave her the money to pay her debts.'

He paused once more for a drink. 'Well,' he went on, 'about a month after that, they were all eating together, Waltz and Mrs Thomas and the boy, Reiney Petrasch, when Waltz decided to open up and tell them where the gold came from. He told them how he and Weiser had met Don Miguel Peralta and gone to the mine, and about the deal that was done afterwards so that the mine became theirs. He told how he and his partner had gone back and mined there, saying that they'd hidden the ore they took out in three caches nearby. He had gone off for supplies, just like Weiser had told Doc Walker, but he'd delayed for some reason or another and got back to the mine a day late. He'd found the place wrecked and his partner's bloody shirt with an arrow hole in it, and he reckoned Weiser was dead.'

Braithwaite drew reflectively on his cigar. 'He never knew, you know, that Weiser had escaped. He always blamed himself for Weiser's death. Thinking his partner dead, he lit out of there, opening one of the caches and taking the gold from it with him. All the time since then – nearly twenty years – he'd kept quiet about his gold and the mine. He'd been back once and taken the dust from another cache, but the biggest one was still there. He felt he was getting too old to do anything about the mine, but he reckoned the three of them could make a quick trip there in the spring and clear the last cache, which he said had about twenty thousand dollars' worth of ore in it.'

Our host looked both of us in the face. 'I don't know', he said, 'if you gentlemen believe in bad luck. Maybe not, one of you being a doctor and the other a seeker after facts, but I've seen enough out West to make me wonder. I sometimes reckon that there's some kind of curse on that mine. Nobody who has to do with it gets any real good out of it, and that was the way with Waltz. It was all fixed up for them to make their trip in the spring of ninety-one. He was going to show them the mine itself, so that if they ever wanted to work it they'd know where it was, but that wasn't the way things worked out.' He shook his head.

'What happened?' I asked.

'Well, in March of that year the Salt and the Verde rivers overflowed and Phoenix had a great flood. Poor old Waltz was flooded and got sick. Helena Thomas and Reiney nursed him, but he died, without being able to take them to the mine.' He stopped and looked in both our faces again, as though seeking to know if we had believed him.

'This is all very interesting, Major,' observed Holmes, 'and I see your implication that Crosby and Indian Tommy shipped gold from the Peralta mine across the Atlantic, but you must admit that the mine's very existence rests on two pieces of hearsay.'

'Hearsay you might call it,' said the American, 'and I suppose that, rightly, it is, but I had Weiser's story from the post doctor at Camp Grant who knew Doc Walker, and Mrs Thomas told me Waltz's story herself. Now, she'd never heard Weiser's story, but the two halves fit together, don't they?'

'They do indeed,' agreed Holmes, 'but it is, nevertheless, only two stories.'

'Well, now,' Braithwaite continued, 'if Dr Watson will just touch the bell for another drink, I think I can tell you about others who found the Peralta mine. Most of them lived to regret it, though not very long. Added to which, gentlemen, there's a very particular reason why this story fits with the one you told me.'

Chapter Sixteen

Finders and Losers

Our glasses were refilled, cigars had circulated and I looked expectantly to our host to continue his narrative. He was gazing in perplexity at Sherlock Holmes. My friend lay sprawled in his chair, his head thrown against its back, his cigar in one corner of his mouth and his long fingers steepled in front of his face. I could not tell if his eyes were open or closed. 'Pray continue, Major,' he said, with no expression of face or voice.

Braithwaite turned a bemused glance on me, then launched anew into his narrative: 'What I've told you is only the history of those who seemed to have some kind of right to the Peralta mine – Don Miguel himself and the two Dutchmen – but there are others who seem to have had dealings with it. For example, before Weiser and Waltz worked it, old prospectors and miners in Arizona used to call it "Doc Thorne's Mine".'

' "Doc Thorne's Mine",' I repeated. 'Why was that?'

'Well, back just after the war there was a post doctor at Fort McDowell called Thorne. He was a young man, not long qualified, and his friend Kit Carson had persuaded him to take a post with the California Column.'

'Kit Carson?' I said, 'the great frontiersman?'

'The same,' acknowledged Braithwaite. 'Carson held a colonel's rank and he was also Indian Agent for all of New Mexico and Arizona.'

'What was the California Column?' asked Holmes.

'That was the corps of volunteers who took over when the Army withdrew from the south-western forts because of the war. This was all just after the war, when we hadn't got army garrisons back into those forts, so the Column was still at McDowell. Anyhow, Thorne doctored for the Column and he treated the Apaches and their children, and they got so grateful to him that they said they wanted to give him a gift by way of thanking him.'

'They gave him the secret of the Peralta mine?' I said.

'No, Doctor. They took him blindfolded to a place where they let him take off the blindfold. There was a heap of gold ore on the ground – ore so rich that Thorne said there were only a few fragments of stone among it – and they let him take a sack of it away with him. He later sold the contents of that sack in Frisco for about six thousand dollars.'

'But this was not a mine site?' Holmes enquired.

'No, Mr Holmes. It was a canyon in the hills. All Thorne knew was that he saw a rectangle of old stones, like the remains of an old building, while he had the blindfold off and he saw a distinctive peak on the skyline.'

'In what way was it distinctive?' asked my friend.

Braithwaite chuckled. 'Thorne remarked to the Apaches that it looked mighty like the more masculine parts of a stallion, and they laughed and said that was what they called it. Then they had the blindfold on him again and took him back.'

'Why, Major,' said Holmes, 'do you associate this tale with the Peralta mine? Thorne saw only a pile of ore in an anonymous canyon, of which there must be many in the hills and mountains of Arizona.'

'Well, gentlemen, I don't know that Doc Thorne ever said his gold came from the Peralta mine, but there is a connection and it brings me to my friend Teddy Danziger.' He puffed at his cigar for a moment. 'Teddy's by way of being a big man in Phoenix these days, but he's done all manner of things in the past. He was a miner in Montana, I know that for a fact, and who knows what over the years, but just after the war he was keeping a hay ranch at Tulare in California.'

'That's where he met Indian Tommy,' I said, recalling Danziger's telegram.

'Exactly, Doctor,' the American agreed. 'One day there rolled up to Teddy's ranch a boy of about fourteen who was looking for work. Teddy took him on, but he soon noticed two strange things about the boy.'

'What were they?' asked Holmes.

'Well, in the first place, although the boy was American – at least he was white – he spoke very poor, broken English.'

'He might have been of German or Dutch or Spanish parentage,' suggested Holmes.

Our host shook his head. 'No, sir. He told Teddy that he was from Texas, that all of his family had been massacred by the Comanches when he was small and that the Indians had taken him away and raised him among them.'

'Is that a common practice?' Holmes enquired.

'Pretty frequent. I've already told you about Micky Free, but I've seen numbers of white people who've been kidnapped and raised among the Indians. Some of them have come back, but quite a few decided to stay with the Indians when they grew up. Anyhow,' he went on, 'this boy – Indian Tommy, as he became – said that he'd been traded from tribe to tribe. First the Comanches traded him to the Mescalero Apaches, then the

Mescaleros traded him to the Arizona Apaches. Then, when he was about thirteen, the Apaches told him he couldn't stay with the tribe, showed him the way to Prescott and left him to make his own way back among the whites.'

'That', said Holmes, 'suggests that there was something unusual about the boy. The trading from tribe to tribe and the refusal to allow him to grow up within the tribe imply that they found him wanting in some way.'

'My thoughts entirely, Mr Holmes. In the light of what he became, it has crossed my mind that he was too violent and unruly for them, for their children are well brought-up as a rule.'

Holmes nodded and Braithwaite resumed his story. 'It appears that Teddy was sorry for the kid, because after he heard the boy's story he told him he could always have a job and a home with him. So the boy stayed around and that was when folks started calling him "Indian Tommy". Then one day he saw Teddy take some gold nuggets off a miner as a payment and he asked Teddy why he took them. Teddy explained to the kid that gold ore was what money was made from and the kid said he knew two places in Arizona where there was lots of gold ore.'

'One of which was the Peralta mine?' I suggested.

'Don't rush your fences, Doctor. Just let me take things in order. Teddy got all the particulars from the boy and he thought about going after the gold. Before he'd gotten around to it, Indian Tommy announced that he was leaving, said he was going after the gold. Teddy tried to stop him, said that the kid was older and the Apaches would get him, but the kid reckoned he could handle the Apaches and off he went. Teddy thought for a long time that the Apaches had killed the boy, but then he showed up in Tombstone, where he got a reputation for a fast temper and a faster hand.'

'Did Danziger ever go after the mine?' I asked.

Braithwaite nodded. 'He did eventually. About sixty-eight or nine he sold the California ranch and moved to Arizona. Then he led a party to one of the places the kid had told him about. Well, the boy was right. When they got there, they found that the site was already being worked and most of the best locations were. They pegged a site and worked it, but they were only taking less than twenty dollars a day, so they gave up. Turned out that the place was what they called Rich Hill. That mine produced hundreds of thousands of dollars' worth.' He shook his head reflectively.

'So, the boy was telling the truth,' I remarked.

'I reckon so,' he agreed, 'and Teddy Danziger thought the same. Later on he persuaded two of his partners to come with him and look for the second mine the kid had told about. Now, Indian Tommy had told Teddy that the second mine was near a big peak that stuck up, and Teddy asked around to see what anyone knew about such a mountain. He was told there were two such peaks in the Superstition Mountains – Sombrero Butte and Weaver's Needle.' He shook his head sadly. 'They picked Sombrero Butte and it all went wrong. Before they got there the Apaches jumped them and they had to fight for their lives. Well, they beat off the Apaches, but Teddy was in a terrible state. In the fighting his shotgun had gone off by accident and smashed his right leg, so his partners put him on his horse and got him into Fort McDowell. It took them three days and Teddy was near dead, but they got him to the post surgeon.'

'Not Dr Thorne?' I said.

'No, Doctor. This was about eighty-one and Thorne was long gone. His successor looked at Teddy's leg and told him that he was going to lose it, that the bone was all smashed and the wound was infected, but Teddy wouldn't have it. He said he'd rather die than lose his leg. So the surgeon did his best. He stopped the infection, but then he told Teddy that he was crippled for life.

He told him never to walk without a cane or a crutch and not to walk on rough ground, not even up and down any steps or stairs.'

Again he shook his head reflectively and I thought about Danziger's terrible injury, made worse by heat and infection and movement. I was amazed that he had lived, let alone walked again. 'What has become of him?' I enquired.

'Oh, he's done well enough for himself, crippled or not. He owns a big piece of Phoenix now and gets richer every day.'

'You were going to tell us', Sherlock Holmes suddenly interrupted, 'of the second strange thing about Indian Tommy. The first was his speech.'

'That's right,' agreed Braithwaite, 'so I was, but I got kind of sidetracked by Teddy Danziger's story. Well, now, the other strange thing about the kid was that he had scars all over his back – not just natural scars from an old injury, but a pattern of scars that seemed to have been drawn with a knifepoint.'

Sherlock Holmes opened his eyes wide, clenched his teeth on his pipe and sat forward to pick up his glass. 'So there is really very little doubt that the man we first heard referred to as Teddy Danziger – the American who crewed on Crosby's yacht – was, in fact, Indian Tommy.'

'It certainly seems so,' agreed our host, smiling. 'I was beginning to think you weren't very taken by my story, Mr Holmes.'

Holmes shook has head. 'No, no,' he said. 'You will allow, Major, that in pursuit of gold any alleged ore must be put to an acid test, I'm sure. Well, the pursuit of accurate data is also a question of mining nuggets of what may be valuable and testing them to ascertain their purity'.

Braithwaite grinned. 'And do my samples pass muster?' he asked.

'There are still difficulties,' Holmes answered. 'We can, I think, agree that the American who crewed for Crosby and who was murdered in Wales is Indian Tommy.'

The Major and I nodded and Holmes went on: 'That raises a strong tendency to believe that what he persuaded Crosby to ship to England was gold from an American mine. That is a perfectly reasonable possibility, more than that – a good possibility. What is not clear is that it is from the Peralta mine and, even if it is, why that should provoke someone into crossing the Atlantic to exact revenge.'

The American puffed at his cigar. 'Yes,' he said slowly, 'I understand what you say, but I don't quite follow why you say that the gold may not be from the Peralta mine.'

'Let us accept', invited Holmes, 'that there is, somewhere in the mountains of Arizona, a rich gold mine, deeded by Don Miguel Peralta to the two Dutchmen. Let us accept that Dr Thorne received the bounty of the Apaches in gold ore, though not, it seems, from a mine site. Let us accept that Indian Tommy knew of two such sites and that, as events occurred, his information was proved correct in one instance. You do not establish that the mine deeded by Don Miguel and the mine described by Indian Tommy are the same, let alone that Thorne's golden reward came from the same mine.'

The American looked puzzled for a moment, then light broke in his eyes and he slapped his thigh and chuckled heartily. 'I beg your pardon, gentlemen, I really do,' he exclaimed. 'I must be getting old, or it's the ocean voyage. I guess I prefer sailing ships. These steam things are too fast altogether. There's no time to reflect before you get where you're going and you don't know what time it is.'

'It is about eight hours ahead of the time in Arizona,

I imagine,' remarked Holmes. 'Do I take it that you have overlooked some element in your narrative?'

'You could say so, Mr Holmes. You could say so. While you told your story I listened and sorted out in my mind the things I knew that connected with it, but I guess I left one out. When I talked to Mrs Thomas, she told me what Waltz had said to her about the mine. He told her it was in sight of Weaver's Needle.'

Holmes sank back into his chair, a smile of gratification lightening his features. 'Ah!' he exclaimed. 'Now we have a chain of connections.' And he struck off the items, one by one, with his right hand against the fingers of his left. 'The Peralta mine is within sight of Weaver's Needle – Dr Thorne was taken to a pile of ore within sight of a mountain that stuck up on the skyline – Indian Tommy described such a mountain to Edmund Danziger. Now we have reasonably established that Crosby's American and Indian Tommy are one and the same, it does seem likely that Indian Tommy's cargo, which he persuaded Crosby to ship, was gold from the Peralta mine.'

Braithwaite smiled. 'I am pleased to have been of assistance,' he said, 'but think I can tell you a little more. I haven't mentioned yet the question of missing heads.'

Chapter Seventeen

Headhunters

The ability of Sherlock Holmes to absorb quantities of alcohol without the drug showing the least effect on his behaviour or his intellectual processes is only one of the many phenomena I have observed in him over the years, but it is so pronounced as to make him a physiological marvel.

Both Braithwaite and I were beginning to suffer from the amount of alcohol we had taken and, despite Holmes's urgent interest in the American's new information, I insisted on a break while strong coffee was ordered, a suggestion which met with no opposition from our host.

Once our coffee had been poured, Holmes leaned forward urgently. 'You were about to tell us about "missing heads",' he reminded the Major.

'So I was. Well, now, this story goes back about thirteen or fourteen years. In the summer of eighty or eighty-one, I forget exactly when, two youngsters showed up at the Silver King mine, near Pinal, looking for work. They saw Aaron Mason, who managed the mine and the mill there, and they told him they were

123

ex-army, that they'd just finished their time at Fort McDowell. They could have gone home, but they'd decided to stay out West and be cowboys. Then they heard that mining paid better, so they wanted to give it a try. Well, they had no mining experience, but Mason liked the look of them, so he set them on as labourers at the mill. Then they told him a remarkable story. They said that, coming from Fort McDowell, they'd taken what they reckoned would be a short cut as they'd known the area when they were soldiering, but it had turned out rougher than they expected. Nevertheless, they'd struck lucky on the way.' He stirred his coffee and took a long draught. 'They showed Mason a sack of ore and told him they'd had it from an old abandoned mine they came across on their way.'

'The Peralta mine?' I asked, but Braithwaite ignored me.

'Well,' he went on, 'Mason looked at what they'd got and told them that it was sorted ore of a very high grade and they'd got about seven or eight hundred dollars' worth. He offered to have it assayed and give them a price for it, and he told them that, if they knew where that mine was, they'd be wasting their time working at the mill, they should go back and claim the old mine.'

Braithwaite lit another cigar and sipped at his coffee. 'They said they could find their way back to the mine and that there was so much ore there you could fill a wagon bed with it, a statement which Mason didn't give much credit. As a professional mining man, I guess he was too well used to amateurs who'd found the greatest lode in the area. Still,' he continued, 'Mason was struck by the quality of the ore they'd brought in, so they made a three-way deal among them that they'd register a claim to the mine and he'd be a partner with them, supplying the mining expertise. He had their ore assayed at about seven hundred dollars and paid it over, so they could afford to set themselves up, and they agreed to go back to the mine and set out the necessary legal notices for two claims side by side. They bought their equipment and supplies, and set out from Pinal after dark, with a couple of burros to carry all their gear. Mason reckoned, on what they had told him, that their mine was somewhere around Weaver's Needle, and he calculated that they should be maybe two days going and two days coming, so he'd expect them back in Pinal in no more than ten days at worst.'

He stared thoughtfully into his coffee cup, but didn't drink. 'The last anybody saw of them two boys alive was when they set out from Pinal,' he said.

'What became of them?' I asked.

He shook his head. 'Nobody knows for certain. They hadn't made it back to Pinal in ten days and Aaron Mason got worried about them. When it ran out to two weeks, he reckoned the Apaches had got them, so he set out with about twenty men to look for them, but search as they did, they never found a trace. Mason got to wondering if he'd been wrong about Weaver's Needle. It crossed his mind that it just might have been Tortilla Mountain that the boys had seen, which is another, similar, sort of peak about six miles from Weaver's Needle. He decided to have a search there, when he ran into a cattleman who knew the canyons near Weaver's Needle, so Mason asked him if he'd take a couple of cowboys in and look around. That was a good thought, gentlemen, because the cowboys found one of them.'

'How was he found?' asked Holmes.

'He was dead – of course. Shot by a rifle and lying naked just off a trail south of the Superstition Mountains.'

'Naked!' I exclaimed.

'Naked,' he repeated. 'That's an Apache trick, to take a victim's clothes. They strip them before death if they mean to torture them, or afterwards if they kill them quick. They always take the clothing and any gear at all.

125

Mules and burros they take for food, and horses they take to ride or trade. But something else was missing as well. They never found his head.'

He paused and I remembered poor Crosby's remains in the mortuary beside the Thames.

'Then how was he identified?' asked Holmes. 'Having neither head nor clothing must have made it difficult.'

'So it was,' agreed our host, 'but they did find a hat a few yards away from the body. It was an old army hat and Mason reckoned it was the hat that one of the youngsters had worn when he saw them.'

Holmes nodded. 'Was there', he asked, 'any indication of how the head had been removed?'

Braithwaite looked at him coolly across his coffee cup for a moment. 'Mr Holmes, you are talking about a body that had been lying in the Arizona sun in summer for several days, not to mention interfered with by animals.'

'Of course, of course,' said Holmes. 'Forgive me, Major, but if there had been any indication it would have been helpful, perhaps.'

'I would guess', said the American, 'that it would have been taken with a hunting knife. How were the ones in England removed?'

'In the one case that we have been able to examine,' answered my friend, 'it is Watson's opinion that something like an axe was used. It is my view that the weapon was wielded by a left-handed man.'

Braithwaite nodded. 'They could have taken an axe from the boys' supplies. I guess they'd have had one, but they're more likely to have used a hunting knife.'

'What became', I asked, 'of the second lad? You said that neither of them was seen alive.'

'That's so, Doctor. For a while after they buried the first one there was a bit more searching about Weaver's Needle, but they never found anything, so in the end they gave up. We asked friendly Apaches if they knew anything, but they either didn't know or they weren't saying. It may have been the latter. I've never gotten a word out of an Apache about the Peralta mine. If they'll talk about it at all they only say it's just a story made up by mad white men.'

'The winter came in and nobody had found the second boy, though it was pretty certain that the Apaches had killed him too. Then, early in the next year, an army patrol chased a party of Apaches into the Superstitions. They lost them in the mountains, but on the way back they found some bones at a place where they camped. There wasn't much left, but this time there was one bit of the clothing: a broken belt with a buckle and it was a United States Army buckle, without a doubt. Well, there were no soldiers missing about there and no ex-soldiers anyone knew about except one, and that was the kid from Pinal.'

'I take it the skull was missing,' remarked Holmes.

'Indeed it was, Mr Holmes, and that, together with the army belt, convinced most people as to who it was had been found.'

Holmes poured himself another cup of coffee and sipped it thoughtfully for a while. 'What do you make of all this, Major?' he asked.

'What do I make of it? Well, now, Mr Holmes, I reckon that there's a rich lode somewhere in the Superstitions that the Apaches have known about for a very long time. Whether they discovered it before Don Miguel's ancestors I couldn't say – perhaps not. Perhaps the Spanish discovered it and the Indians resent white men working it because it's on territory they think of as their own. Maybe they worked it themselves and they don't want white men taking gold from it.'

'What would happen if they tried to work it themselves, Major?' asked Holmes.

'It wouldn't be possible, Mr Holmes. They have no rights as citizens so they couldn't file a claim. If any

Apache tried to sell ore from the mine, he'd be in deep trouble. If he wasn't accused of stealing it, he'd have to explain where he got it, and soon there'd be prospectors all over the Superstitions and a mining town growing up like Tombstone. That's probably what the Apaches are trying to stop.'

Holmes nodded. 'That explains why they kill those who try to find or work the mine,' he agreed, 'and it explains why they have hunted down Indian Tommy and the man who helped him ship his gold, but it leaves something unexplained. Tell me – if you know – when the cowboys found the ex-soldier's body, was there any indication that he had been tortured?'

'Not so far as I know, Mr Holmes. I only heard that his head was missing and he had been shot with a rifle.'

'That must have discouraged people from seeking the mine,' I suggested.

'Not at all,' said Braithwaite. 'I reckon there's no human folly greater than the lust for gold. Nothing stops them. Just a few months after those two kids died another man reckoned he'd found the Peralta mine. He was a fellow who worked at the Silver King, and he showed a rich nugget around and said he'd come across an abandoned mine in the hills, but he never lived to profit by it.'

'What happened to him?' asked Holmes.

'He was crushed in an accident at the mill. I told you – talking about the Peralta mine could make you believe there's a curse on it.'

Holmes drained his coffee, stood up and drew out his watch. 'Major Braithwaite,' he said. 'Watson and I have trespassed upon your good nature and your hospitality for far too long, not to mention picking your brains. You have, I believe, been of considerable help in clarifying some of the inferences which I was drawing. I thank you for your assistance and I ask you, on my behalf, to thank Edmund Danziger for putting us in communication.'

Braithwaite smiled. 'It has been no trespass at all, Mr Holmes. Your colleague will tell you that there is nothing old soldiers enjoy more than shooting the breeze about places where they've soldiered. This evening has been a great pleasure. I have met the most distinguished detective of the age and enjoyed such an evening as I never knew.'

The old soldier's compliment brought a smile to Holmes's lips. 'You are very kind, Major Braithwaite,' he said, 'but Watson and I really must bid you goodnight now and thank you for your hospitality.'

Chapter Eighteen

The Barons of the Colorados

As Holmes and I settled into our hansom on the way back to Baker Street I remarked on the affability of our host.

'A charming fellow indeed, Watson,' said Holmes, 'and his data will be very useful to us.'

'Really? I had thought that you were not particularly impressed by the standard of his evidence.'

'I admit that I could wish that rather less of it were hearsay, Watson, but against that one must put the fact that so much of his information hangs together – both with other items he divulged and with what we already know.'

'I was struck by several of the places he mentioned,' I said, 'such as Weaver's Needle, Silver King and the Superstition Mountains. They are evidently connected with Mrs Crosby's document.'

'So they are,' he agreed. 'It seems likely that the document is no more than the legend which should be attached to a map, and that the map is most likely to be a map of the Peralta mine's location. You will recall that I believed it was only a key to something else.'

'I recall you saying that you thought Peralta was a name. You were right about that.'

'I also said that I should recognise the name's associations. I now do and that forms a part of the confirmation of Braithwaite's stories.'

'In what way?' I asked.

'Did you ever hear, or do you recall, Watson, the affair of the Baron of the Colorados?'

'I cannot say that I have heard the title before.'

'The title was created in 1748 by King Ferdinand VI of Spain, to reward a Spanish citizen for some signal favour to his crown. The citizen in question was one Don Miguel Peralta, and with it went a grant of nearly four thousand square miles of land in the south-western part of North America – most, in fact, of what is now the Territory of Arizona.'

'Astonishing!' I exclaimed. 'Even by the standards of Imperial Spain, that must have been an enormous gift.'

'It was and it was not,' said Holmes. 'While the area was large, it consisted of a wilderness of desert and mountains, peopled by fierce savages. It was not, at that time, a particularly profitable area. Nevertheless, Peralta was determined to hold it, for when Ferdinand was succeeded by Charles III, he sought reaffirmation of his title and of the land grant. This was given and both passed to his son, Don Enrico Peralta. It is not, I think, an unreasonable suggestion that Don Enrico was, in turn, the ancestor of the Don Miguel who deeded the mine to the two Dutchmen.'

'My word,' I said. 'Did they acquire thereby the title of Baron of the Colorados?'

'No, Watson. They were, apparently, only given the rights in the mine. In any case, the United States does not recognise baronies.'

'What a shame,' I said.

'However,' he continued, 'the United States, when it

ratified the Treaty of Guadaloupe Hidalgo at the end of the Mexican War, did agree to recognise all existing grants of land in the territories which it acquired.'

'So', I said, 'the Mexican who gave the Dutchman the mine was the real Baron of the Colorados and owned four thousand miles of Arizona.'

'Most probably,' he agreed. 'But Don Miguel seems to have been a remarkably short-sighted man. Failing to recognise the enormous value of his land grant in an area that was now being settled and developed, in which ranching and mining were taking place, timber being cut, coal being dug and so on, he concentrated only on extracting gold from the ancestral mine and even that he found too dangerous for his taste.'

I shook my head. 'Astonishing. Fancy throwing away such an inheritance. But how do you come to know all this?'

'Because, if Don Miguel failed to recognise that his inheritance was now worth a hundred million dollars, someone else did not. That man was James Reavis, who set out to perpetrate the most cunning and impudent fraud of this century.'

'What did he do?' I asked.

'Reavis travelled America, Mexico and Spain, researching the history of the Peralta family and their royal grant. Then, about twenty-five years ago, he announced that he was the hereditary Baron of the Colorados and demanded rents and royalties from every farm, ranch, mine and manufactory on the Peralta territory in Arizona.'

'But how could he prove it?'

'He was well armed with attested copies of ancient Spanish documents from archives in the Old and New Worlds, which appeared to establish his claim beyond a peradventure. He so terrified the citizens of Arizona that some made accommodations with him and agreed to meet his demands.'

132

'Obviously he was caught.'

'So he was,' said Holmes. 'He had failed to learn a lesson that is ignored by most criminals, from the smallest to the greatest – not to make your demands unrealistically large. Reavis's claim so threatened the prosperity of the territory that, despite his impressive documentation, the authorities simply decided that he must be proved fraudulent. With that in mind, they refused to accept his attested copies of documents and sent their own people to examine the originals, wherever they lay.' He smiled reminiscently. 'His preparation had been enormous and finely detailed but, as is so often the case, his great enterprise was brought to an end by a simple oversight. Many of the forged documents he had placed in old archives passed muster, but in one old Spanish church ledger he had removed a page and tipped in a forged one bearing an extra entry, which showed a ceremony that had never taken place. His forged page was accepted as genuine until the detective noticed that the entries on it did not match the index at the back of that ledger. Further examinations revealed that some of his ancient Spanish documents were written on paper made in Wisconsin. James Reavis – who turned out to be a former conductor of horse trams – ended in prison and the title of Baron of the Colorados seems to have lapsed with the late Don Miguel Peralta. That is why I knew the name and why I should have recalled its connections with Arizona.'

'So it seems likely that there really is a fabulous gold mine somewhere in the Superstition Mountains,' I remarked.

'Very likely. And from Major Braithwaite's information we know that its location is fiercely guarded by the Apaches.'

'Which is why, when Indian Tommy, or whatever his name was, extracted gold from the mine and persuaded

Crosby to ship it to Britain, they sent someone after them, to wreak their vengeance,' I commented.

My friend shook his head vigorously. 'No, Watson, no! I feared that you had taken too much of Major Braithwaite's hospitality and it seems I was right.'

'Well, why, then, did our Apache kill Crosby and the American? Not only kill them – he tortured them!'

'Precisely, Watson! He tortured them.'

I was growing a little irritated. 'I entirely fail to see your point.'

'Consider', he said, 'the stories which Braithwaite retailed to us. The Dutchmen went with Peralta to the mine, extracted a large quantity of gold and returned safely to Mexico.'

'But that is because they were a large and well-armed party,' I protested.

'Of course. But they were not pursued into Mexico. It was only when the Dutchmen were back in Arizona, at the mine, that the Apaches attacked them. The two ex-soldiers – they took gold from the mine with impunity. They were not followed to Pinal and murdered. It was only when they returned to the mountains that they were killed and decapitated. The fellow who found the mine afterwards – he died in a mill accident. He was not pursued and tortured. Do you not now see my thinking?'

It may be that he was right and alcohol had slowed my brain, but I really could not grasp the line of his thought and I said so.

'My point, Watson, is a simple one. The violence of the Apaches has been directed against those who sought to work the mine, in order to prevent them. They have not gone on to pursue vengeance against them, except in the case of Crosby and Indian Tommy. Therefore, it is not the simple act of taking gold from the mine that has sent our killer five thousand miles. Nor, if it were, would he have tried twice to kill me.'

'Then what does he want?' I asked.

'I told you that Mrs Crosby's document was a key from which we should be able to define the nature of the lock,' he began.

'Actually,' I protested, 'you said that it was possible to define the nature of a key from the lock which it must fit.'

'The reverse applies,' he snapped. 'We now know that Crosby's document is a key to a map of the Peralta mine. It is that map which our killer seeks – a map which, if it is not destroyed, will bring into the Superstition Mountains the horde of white gold seekers that the Indians fear. That is why he tortured Crosby and the American. That is why he has sought to kill me. Having learned of my investigations into the matter – most probably through our visit to Graby – he thinks we may know the whereabouts of the map.'

'You really believe so?'

'It is obvious,' he replied. 'If he were here simply to exact revenge on Crosby and Indian Tommy, he would have gone home, satisfied. If I thought that was his motive, I would have revealed all my findings to Lestrade and told him that his perpetrator was somewhere in Arizona.'

'How can you be sure that he has not gone home?' I asked.

'Because his attempts to kill me were after he had killed both Crosby and the American, Watson. He will not – cannot – return until he has recovered the map.'

'But you don't have it,' I protested.

'No,' he agreed, 'but I am pretty certain that I know where it is and, if I am right, I shall very soon have it.'

'How are you going to get it?'

'I am going, early tomorrow morning, to don my workman's garb and join the queues of casual labourers who wait for hire in the docks.'

And that was the last word he would say on the matter.

Chapter Nineteen

A Deadly Warning

If my mind had been dulled after our evening with Major Braithwaite, it was still not at its best the next morning. By the time I rose, Holmes had breakfasted and left the house, dressed, as Mrs Hudson informed me, 'like a common workman'.

I made a leisurely breakfast and settled down to pass the time with the morning papers. In Holmes's absence I always missed his acerbic or illuminating comments on items in the press and used to wonder what he would make of certain stories. I find that I still do it now, some twenty years after leaving Baker Street. By mid-morning I had exhausted the newspapers without finding much to interest me and nothing that I thought would attract Holmes's attention. I sat and smoked and, unbidden, my mind turned back upon the events of the previous evening.

I rehearsed in my mind the various tales of the Peralta mine which Braithwaite had told us and ran over Holmes's analysis of them. I saw that his propositions had a good deal of reason in them and it suddenly occurred to me that, according to his own arguments, Holmes himself was now the target of the Apache assassin and that, by venturing into the docks, he was bringing himself closer to a ferocious and cunning adversary whose intention in remaining in England was to take my friend's life. Through the four decades of my acquaintance with Sherlock Holmes I have never once known him flinch from any danger. I have long considered him the bravest man I have ever known, but my reflections caused me no little unease. Braithwaite had made clear to us both the ferocity of the Apaches and their extreme skill and cunning, and it would need only a little good fortune on the part of Holmes's adversary to swing the advantage against my friend.

It occurred to me also that, in identifying Holmes as a person who might well be in possession of the Peralta map, the Apache must, inevitably, be aware of my connection with Holmes and must thereby regard me as a legitimate target of his hostility. I do not put myself forward as an inordinately courageous man, but I think I can honestly say that I have never hesitated to accompany Holmes into whatever potential danger threatened him. Nevertheless I was gratified by the thought that I, at least, was reasonably securely ensconced in our sitting room, made more secure by Holmes's insistence that our windows be fitted with complicated locks. He, on the other hand, was somewhere in the docks, perhaps in cheek-by-jowl proximity with the Indian.

These reflections made me profoundly uneasy all day, so that I could not settle to read and did not wish to leave the premises, not from fear but from a belief that Holmes might wish to call upon my assistance at some point.

It was early evening when I heard my friend's foot upon the stair and opened the door to find a grubby labourer upon our landing. Holmes greeted me warmly, then looked about him at the books and periodicals I had picked up, glanced at briefly and put down throughout the day, as well as the fug of tobacco smoke that I had generated. 'If I did not know that, however well disguised, I have spent a long day humping sides of meat on the docks, Watson, I would swear that the smoky atmosphere and disordered state of this room was proof that I have been here all day. I take it that you have not been out to the park or the Billiards Room?'

I did not admit to him the reasons why I had remained indoors. 'It seems to me', I said, a touch more sharply than I had intended, 'that when a homicidal savage is seeking to rob and murder you, it is a bad time to be sauntering about in public unnecessarily, let alone loitering about the very place where the killer works.'

He lifted one eyebrow and looked at me without comment, while he began to pull the false whiskers from his face, before towelling away the paint that had helped his disguise. 'Do I take it', he said, as he dropped into the basket chair and reached for the Persian slipper in which he kept his tobacco, 'that you do not approve of my expedition to the docks?'

'I do not,' I confirmed. 'You have seen what this man can do. Braithwaite has told us of the skill and savagery of the tribe. He has already penetrated this very room and sought to trap one or other of us with his deadly reptile, and he came within a hand's breadth of killing you at Eacham, yet you feel it necessary to set yourself up against him by going down to the docks. The kind of man that Major Braithwaite describes will have preternaturally sharp eyes and finely responsive senses. Despite your admitted skills at disguise, Holmes, can you be absolutely sure that he has not identified you?'

He chuckled quietly. 'I am touched by your concern for me, old friend, but there are things I need to know and the only place to find them is in and about the docks.'

'What things are they?' I asked.

'In the first place, as I told Lestrade the other evening,

there is still no case against the Apache which would stand up in an English court. You and I may be satisfied that I have read the clues aright and correctly deduced the story behind events and the reasons for the killings. Even Lestrade, who often seems to think that my successes arise from long chains of fortunate coincidence, appears to agree with me in this case, but we still lack evidence of a kind that will convince a jury.'

An even more ominous thought struck me. 'You are surely not', I protested, 'placing yourself close to this man in order to provoke him into some rash act?'

'Watson,' he said, 'if I try to face up to the dangers that arise in an enquiry, that is because danger is an inescapable element of my singular profession. I do not court it, but I will not turn from it. On the other hand, I have as good a respect for my own skin as any man and will not place myself in peril without sufficient reason. Will it help to assure you that my danger is not so great as you fear, if I tell you that my working partner throughout today has been a monosyllabic foreign labourer, known on the docks as "The Spaniard", who is, in fact, the object of enquiry?'

It did nothing of the sort. 'You have been working right alongside him!' I almost shouted. 'Is that not the veriest folly?'

'Certainly not,' he said. 'The Spaniard comes in for a good deal of hard treatment on the docks, from both the overseers and his fellow labourers, because of his apparent shortcomings in language. He sees me only as one of his less offensive colleagues – a simple Irishman, a former sailor who has picked up a word or two of Spanish, but whose simplicity makes him also the butt of others' humour and insult – wherefore, if he does not welcome working with me, he finds it easier than any other pairing and pays me less watchful attention.'

I was not convinced. I still believed that he was playing an unnecessarily dangerous game. 'And what information do you hope to get which will make a case against him?' I asked.

'I want to know where he lives,' said Holmes. 'He appears among the casual labourers at the dock gate each morning, clad very much as they are and carrying nothing, yet we know that he must have some kind of a bolt-hole somewhere in that vicinity.'

'How do we know that?' I enquired.

'Watson, Watson,' he complained. 'Where did he take Crosby and hold him during the time that he tortured him? You could not do that in a dockside tavern, nor even the lowest doss-house in the East End. Where did he keep the poisonous Percy after he purchased him? His pet was not, I think you will agree, one that could be carried about in the pocket like a schoolboy with a mouse. Where, in fact, does he keep his weapons? For I have seen none about him at the docks.'

'And if you find his lair,' I said, 'how will that assist in proving a case against him?'

'You are still not at your best, Watson. You, yourself, have seen the arrow which was fired at me. No doubt he has others of the same distinctive type. The possession of those alone would be sufficient cause for Lestrade to arrest him, though I have no intention of permitting that until I have a far better case against him. I must find his fortress, Watson, for there will be evidence there. Braithwaite told us that Apaches always strip their victims. So he did, but where are the clothes he took from Indian Tommy and poor Crosby? They too may be still in his possession.'

'How will you find his home?'

'I shall follow him,' he said.

'And suppose he were to become suspicious of the affable Irishman who labours alongside him,' I postulated. 'What if he turns the tables on you and follows his Irish colleague, only to discover that he lives at 221b Baker Street?'

'Really, Watson, I understand and appreciate your concern for my safety, but you do not have to treat me as a complete simpleton. While I might be at his advantage in the Superstition Mountains, he is on my territory here. I can assure you that I have taken every precaution against being followed back here, not least so as to afford you as much protection as possible.'

I did not, at first, understand how I had begun as an exponent of an argument and suddenly found myself one of its subjects, and it disturbed me. With another man I would have suspected guile, but not in Sherlock Holmes. Whether he had intended the effect or not, I found myself unwilling to press my argument now that the suggestion hung between us that I might be self-serving. Perhaps I reacted with too much sensitivity, but the situation destroyed my appetite. Holmes, on the other hand, sat to the dinner table with enthusiasm and ate heartily, maintaining a flow of affable chatter meanwhile.

As he laid down his cutlery and put away his napkin he looked across at me. 'Watson, Watson,' he scolded. 'This really will not do! You have barely touched your food. You are in grave danger of upsetting Mrs Hudson.'

In another frame of mind I might have reflected with amusement on the many occasions when I had sat and watched Holmes, his mind entirely taken up with some obscure and difficult train of thought, picking at or completely ignoring the excellent cuisine of our landlady, but I was not in a humorous mood. 'I do not seem to have any appetite.'

'Watson,' he said seriously, 'I am, as ever, touched by your evident concern for my well-being, but I fear you do me less than justice. Our opponent may be wily and ferocious, but those are qualities which I believe I can emulate and – again – he has the disadvantage that he is not defending his native mountains; he is attacking on my territory. I promise you that I shall give his nature and his skills the respect they undoubtedly deserve, but if I wait for Scotland Yard to deal with him I shall wait for ever. As to your appetite, Watson, we must do something about it.' And, picking up one of the newspapers I had left scattered on the sofa, he began to scan its columns eagerly.

'A little music, I think. Let us refresh the mind and spirit this evening, eh, Watson?'

I have rarely felt less like an evening at a concert hall but there was no gainsaying Holmes. In a very short space of time he had me changed and accompanying him to a concert. What the works performed were or, indeed, who were the soloists, I cannot recall. I do, however, remember that Holmes sat throughout the performance with his head flung back and his eyes half closed, the long fingers of his right hand extended and moving gently with the music's rhythm, the very portrait of a man without a care in the world, rather than one who had chosen to pit himself against a fierce and cunning opponent who sought his life. Strangely, my friend's prescription began to take effect and I found myself increasingly carried away by the music, so that when, as we left the hall, Holmes suggested a late supper, I assented gladly.

An excellent meal at Romanov's restored me almost completely, so that I was in a far more optimistic frame of mind when we dropped from our hansom cab in Baker Street. Mrs Hudson had long retired and I waited while Holmes reached in his coat pocket for his key to the front door. A moment later I heard a faint jingle on the steps and Holmes, with a mild exclamation, stooped to retrieve the dropped key. In the same instant something flew silently past my head and embedded itself deeply in the varnished wood of our front door. I cried aloud and turned and, as I did so, a second missile followed the first, finding its mark alongside its precursor. The street, so far as I could see, was empty, apart from our departing hansom at the far end but, as I peered about me, a dark figure detached itself from the shadows of a doorway on the opposite side and darted away. For a moment our attacker appeared under a street lamp and I was able to catch a glimpse of a shortish, darkly clad figure, with black hair that caught the lamp's light for an instant before he plunged into the shadows beyond and vanished into a side street.

I sprang away from our doorstep but Holmes seized my arm and firmly restrained me. 'It would be a waste of effort, Watson. There are mews opening from both sides of that street. You would never catch him. Even if you did, this is not the time or place to confront him.'

I looked at the two leather-handled daggers, still quivering in our door, and considered how easily the first would have taken Holmes in the back as lifted his key to the lock and how readily the second would have taken me as I stepped towards my friend.

Chapter Twenty

Pictures Without Words

I found myself alone when I rose on the next morning and at first I feared that Holmes had taken himself off to the docks again. The two daggers lay on our sitting-room table, where Holmes had dropped them after withdrawing them from the door, and I examined them closely. They were of identical type but slightly different manufacture. Both were handmade, the blades having been hand ground from strips of dull but hard steel, and a vicious edge and point achieved. In each case the handle had been constructed by binding and weaving strips of alternately coloured leather around the upper portion of the metal and a tuft of leather strips hung from the top of the hilt. They were evidently of savage origin and I had no difficulty in believing that they had been manufactured by the Apache or his fellow tribes-men. I am no knife thrower, but even in my hands I was aware of the fine balance that had been imparted to the weapons, so that one sensed they would spring from one's hands with awful accuracy.

I laid them on Holmes's writing desk and shook my head as I wondered at the instinct that had provoked my gloomy mood of the previous day and at the tiny chance that had saved both Holmes and me from these implements of death.

When Mrs Hudson laid breakfast she cheered me slightly by assuring me that Holmes, so far as she was aware, had not gone to the docks and, sure enough, he descended from his room once he heard the clatter of crockery, smiling and rubbing his hands.

'You are not', I asked, 'going to the docks today?' after we had greeted each other.

'Not in my Irish persona, no, Watson. It seems that I have taken your concern for my well-being too much for granted and today I shall try not to worry you. I am going east today, but I shall be pleased if you will accompany me. I intend to pay a return call upon Mr Graby.'

Graby's shop had changed not at all since our first visit and, once again, the proprietor stood behind his own counter.

'You will remember me, no doubt,' said Holmes.

'So I do,' said Graby. 'You're the Scotland Yard cove that come after Teddy Danziger. He ain't been back, you know.'

'The consultant to Scotland Yard,' Holmes corrected, 'and the so-called Teddy Danziger will not be coming back.'

'In jail, then, is he?' asked Graby. 'What did you get him for?'

'Your erstwhile lodger is not in jail, Mr Graby,' Holmes replied. 'Most of him is presently reposing in a pauper's grave in north Wales. His head, however, is most probably in the Property Storeroom at Scotland Yard.'

Graby's furtive, flickering eyes bulged and he stared

at my friend. 'His head!' he exclaimed. 'Gordon Bennett! What happened to him?'

'You will, no doubt, recall the dark-skinned man who called here asking for Danziger. It seems that he caught up with him and settled some important grievance.'

Even in the gloom of the shop I could see that, under its patina of oil and dirt, Graby's face had turned chalk-white. 'I ain't in any danger, am I?' he asked. 'I mean, you have got him, haven't you – the bloke as done it?'

'I', said Holmes, 'am not the official police, but I am reasonably confident that they have not arrested your caller, though he works in the docks and lives some-where in this vicinity. However, that is not what brought me back to your shop, Mr Graby. I was wondering if you could supply me with a quantity of grey and black paint, suitable for marine use.'

The chandler seemed to have difficulty in focusing his mind on Holmes's request, but at last he pointed and said, 'Over there, under that tarpaulin, grey and black, first quality, same as they uses on battleships and the Royal Yacht. I could do a special price if you was to want any quantity.'

Holmes strolled in the direction indicated and, with his stick, flicked away a piece of tarpaulin that covered a stack of paint drums. Their sides bore only plainly printed labels indicating the nature of the contents and serial numbers.

Graby followed us over. 'If you want to look,' he said, 'pry the top off one of them. You'll see it's all the best stuff.'

'I'm sure it is, Mr Graby, but I do not need to pry open a drum to see its quality.' He lifted one canister from the stack and turned it over, setting it upside down on the floor. 'Its quality,' he said, 'together with its origin and its intended use is attested by that mark.' And he pointed with his stick at the base of the drum where a black broad arrow mark showed plainly.

'I don't know what you mean, sir,' Graby muttered, and his eyes were downcast and moving fast.

'Come now, Graby,' said Holmes. 'In the marine chandlery business I cannot believe that you are unfamiliar with that mark. Indeed, were I to take the trouble, I'm sure I should find it on the base of every one of these canisters. Since a long-dead Marquis of Winchester chose to use the Paulets' family crest of three spearheads to identify government stores, that simplified form of it has always stood as a mark on goods made for the Crown. Would you care to explain how these items come to be for sale in your shop?'

Graby looked from Holmes to me and back again, his eyes flicking like little flies. 'You're mistaken, sir,' he mumbled. 'They was government issue. They was stored in that big warehouse down in Brewers Lane, not the one as was burned down – the one next to it. Only a part of that one burned and these goods was in it. They're fire damaged, sir – disposal goods.'

Holmes gazed at him steadily. 'Mr Graby,' he said, 'the damaged warehouse in Brewers Lane has not been cleared. As I am sure you well know, it was the lower part of the building that caught fire from its neighbour and is now seriously damaged, making it impossible at present to remove the goods from the upper floors without danger. You have been receiving stolen property, Mr Graby, and stolen property of the Crown at that. I am not certain whether theft of stores from a Royal Naval dockyard is not still a hanging matter.'

Graby's mouth opened and closed several times without a sound emerging, but eventually he managed to croak, 'Isn't there anything I could do for you, sir?'

Holmes smiled warmly. 'Ah!' he exclaimed, 'that's much better.' And he sauntered back towards the counter. 'Perhaps you could begin by telling me the truth about Teddy Danziger, as you called him.'

'I told you the truth, sir,' said Graby, scurrying after Holmes like a fat rat. 'Honest, I did.'

'What you told me may well have been true,' said Holmes, 'but it was certainly not all of the truth. Why did you search the American's room after he was gone?'

Graby gobbled silently again, then muttered, 'He owed me rent, didn't he? I went in to see if he'd left anything of value as I could set off against his dues.'

'And what did you find, Mr Graby?'

'Nothing,' he said, then met Holmes's gaze. 'Well, not much.'

'What was it and where is it?' demanded Holmes.

Graby ducked behind his counter and emerged holding a roll of some material, tied with two pieces of twine. He laid it on the counter top. 'There was only this. I don't even know what it is.'

'Then why did you believe that it might be valuable?' asked Holmes.

'Because he'd hidden it, hadn't he? It was pinned up underneath his table, inside the frame so as you couldn't see it unless you was underneath.'

Holmes took the package and slipped it under his arm. 'Thank you,' he said. 'I shall look after this. In the meantime, if our dark-skinned friend comes calling again, you have my permission to tell him that you gave this package to me. I would not try any of your lies and evasions with him. He is far less well-mannered than I am and has, to my certain knowledge, tortured and murdered two men in order to get his hands on this. Good day, Mr Graby.'

Back at Baker Street, Holmes laid the bundle upon the

sitting-room table and cut the fasteners with his pocket knife, spreading out the material across the table.

It was a sheet of leather, some thirty inches square. Its edges showed marks that suggested it had once been framed and it was possible to see where Indian Tommy had pinned it to the underframe of his table. Its basic colour was a light tan, faded in places, but it had been worked, tooled and tinted with great skill, so as to present a picture, in low relief and in a range of browns and dark reds. I had never seen anything quite like it before, except maybe the decorative landscape pictures produced in China and worked in relief with thread and tiny particles of cork and bark.

'Well, Watson,' Holmes asked, 'what do you make of that?'

Gradually my eyes and brain took in the structure of the elaborate decoration on the table. Basically the picture portrayed a view from above of a considerable area of landscape. At the top and to the left side clusters of mountains were represented, pierced by valleys. Here and there were small groups of houses and an occasional church in the old Spanish style. There were even tiny figures in the landscape. At one point a mule train wound its way up into the mountains and, not far away, another was making its way out into a valley. Scattered all over the picture were clumps of flowers and of the grotesque cactus plants that flourish in America's southwest. These had been delicately cut from thin leather and added to the design by being slipped into slits in the base material.

'It's astonishing, Holmes,' I said. 'I've never seen anything quite like it before. The workmanship is superb and the effect is extremely decorative. Is this really the map of which Braithwaite spoke?'

He nodded. 'This singular creation cannot be other than a map of the Peralta mine's location.'

'But whereabouts in this landscape does the mine appear?'

'That, Watson, is why there is a separate key. To the uninitiated this is merely a decorative panel, fit to hang on any wall. Only the possession of the key will reveal where abouts in the picture lies the Peralta mine.' He rolled the map carefully and laid it on his writing desk. 'Let us take our luncheon, Watson, and afterwards bend our minds to the unlocking of old Don Miguel's secret.'

Holmes ate with a vigour that I had always remarked as indicating a feeling that his enquiries were successful. I admit that I was less gloomy than I had been on the previous day, even though the possession of the Peralta map only emphasised the danger in which we stood.

Once Mrs Hudson had cleared the table, Holmes unrolled the leather map again and drew from his pocket the paper given to him by Mrs Crosby.

A thought crossed my mind and I asked, 'Why did you not mention this paper to Major Braithwaite, even when he referred to names that are listed in it?'

'Caution,' said Holmes. 'On the one hand we have a killer who will stop at nothing to obtain possession of this map. At least Braithwaite possesses no knowledge that might harm him. On the other hand we have, by Braithwaite's own account, a succession of persons who have come to grief through the seeking or finding of the Peralta mine. Gold has a powerful effect upon the minds of even the most balanced persons and I would not have Braithwaite tempted into some indiscretion. However, let us now see how far his information takes us.'

'Well,' I said, 'at the top of the list is the word SUPER-STITIONS, which plainly refers to the range of mountains that he mentioned, and we have SILVER and KING, linked by the same symbol. Could those refer to the mine which he told us about – the Silver King?'

'I imagine that you are right, Watson, and that reveals

a further part of the mechanism. As SILVER and KING are connected by the same symbol, and form a recognisable name, so are WEAVERS and NEEDLE, forming the name of the identifying peak. GREEN and SPRING are similarly connected, and may refer to a place called either Spring Green or Green Spring.'

'What about CANON and BOX?' I asked. 'They don't seem to be a pair, but they are both followed by the square symbol.'

'I suggest that the word is not CANON, but the Spanish form of canyon and the pair refer to what Americans call a "box canyon".'

'Of course,' I agreed, 'but that doesn't seem to be of much help. There are canyons all over the top and right side of this map.'

'So there are,' he said, 'and that brings us to another problem. If this is, as it now appears to be, a list of places and place names within the area of the map – and it is difficult to doubt that in the light of the fact that the only word followed by an X is PERALTA – then another problem arises.'

'What is that?'

'That, unless I am very much mistaken, Watson, not one of these symbols appears anywhere on the entire map.'

I looked, and looked again, but in the end I was forced to admit that he was right.

Chapter Twenty-one

A Plea for Assistance

Holmes was hunched over the map, his meerschaum gripped in his teeth, when I went to bed and I would not have been surprised to find him still in the same pose next morning. Instead, I found him at the breakfast table. 'Have you solved the problem?' I asked him, and nodded to where the leather map lay rolled on his writing desk.

He shook his head. 'No, Watson. For the time being I have abandoned it. What mattered was tracing and acquiring the map. To read its puzzle would be intellectually satisfying, but would not advance our enquiries.'

'It is unlike you to abandon a problem unsolved,' I remarked.

'I shall return to it, but I am not at all sure that its solution will be of any benefit to anyone.'

'An easily worked vein of high-grade gold ore!' I exclaimed. 'I should think someone might benefit from it!'

'The Apaches do not seem to have benefited from it, nor the Peraltas, nor the two Dutchmen, nor the ex-soldiers who found it. Crosby and Indian Tommy died horribly because of it. Would you go seeking the Peralta mine, Watson?'

'Maybe not,' I agreed.

'And you a confirmed gambler,' he twitted me.

'There are some things on which I will not gamble,' I said, rather huffily I admit, for he had touched on a weak point. 'You have reminded me that, even if one were to find the mine, the odds against surviving seem to be pretty heavy.'

I buttered a slice of toast and changed the subject: 'Tell me, are you off to the docks again?'

He shook his head. 'I have an enquiry to pursue in the East End, but I shall avoid the docks.'

He did not invite me to accompany him and I did not press myself upon him. When he desired my presence he always asked. After breakfast he changed, put on his boots and left.

Knowing that he was, at least, not working alongside the Apache made my spirits rather lighter than on the previous occasion when he had left me alone for the day. I took down the leather map and spread it on the dining table once Mrs Hudson had cleared away breakfast, but try as I might, could find nothing in its intricate patterns and illustrations that matched the symbols on Crosby's list. Eventually I put it aside and found a book to amuse me.

I had taken luncheon alone and returned to my book, when Mrs Hudson appeared with a telegram for Holmes. It placed me in a quandary, for it might, I thought, have some bearing on the Crosby case, but I was loath to open it in Holmes's absence. Nevertheless, I thought he could hardly blame me, so I tore it open. It had been sent from Hampshire an hour before and read:

MR SHERLOCK HOLMES STOP BOTH MY SONS ARE ADAMANT

THAT THEY HAVE BEEN STALKED BY SOME MANNER OF SAVAGE IN THE GROUNDS OF OUR HOME THIS MORNING STOP I BELIEVE THEM BUT THE LOCAL POLICE DO NOT TAKE THE MATTER SERIOUSLY STOP PLEASE ASSIST STOP TELE- PHONE BRADON 11 STOP BEATRICE CROSBY

I was appalled. Hastily I scribbled a note to Holmes, packed my Gladstone bag and, leaving the note and the telegram with Mrs Hudson, set out for Waterloo, paus- ing only at a telephone call office to let Mrs Crosby know that I was on my way and to ask for a carriage at the station.

Within an hour of leaving Baker Street I was seated in a train and rattling south-west, but the fastest train would have been too slow. I could not contemplate what I might find by the time I arrived. I knew that Mrs Crosby had household servants, grooms and gardeners, who would defend her, but did not believe for one moment that they were capable of defeating the wily redskin, and I could not drive from my mind the muti- lated remains of poor Crosby and the dreadful paintings of blood in *Gyrfalcon*'s saloon. I sat forward in my seat, trying almost to will the train to travel faster but it stopped, it seemed, at every lamp-post from London into Hampshire. As we journeyed further into the coun- tryside the sunny spring day darkened and sporadic showers streaked the windows of my compartment, while the sky ahead turned to an unnatural watery green, riven by purplish grey banks of cloud.

I was first from the train at Bradon and ran along the platform, but was encouraged to see a dogcart and driver in the station's yard. Its driver introduced himself as Port, Mrs Crosby's groom, and I sprang aboard. Once we had moved off I questioned Port about the situation at Bradon Lodge.

'Well, sir,' he replied, 'I don't rightly know what's happening, sir, but Mrs Crosby rang the big bell at the house after dinner. That's to call us all together at the house if anything goes wrong, like. When we were all together in the kitchen, Mrs Crosby come and talked to us. She said as it wasn't safe for people to be about the garden and the grounds, and we was all to stay in the house till she said as we could go. She had all the men and the boys, sir, like the grooms and gardeners and even young George the bootboy, in the gunroom after that and she gave us all guns. I got a shotgun down by my feet here, sir.'

'Thank you,' I said. 'And by the time you left for the station nothing untoward had taken place?'

'Nothing out of the way as I knows about, sir, but everybody's still there. She said she wouldn't send me to the station on an order, because she said as it might be dangerous, but I said I'd come anyway, seeing as I've got the shotgun.'

I thought how little use his shotgun might be against the silent arrows and knives of our opponent, but I did not enlighten him. 'That was very brave of you,' I said instead. 'I'm sure your mistress appreciates it.'

"Tain't nothing, sir,' he said. 'Mrs Crosby's a good lady to work for and she's had bad enough trouble what with Mr Crosby being killed.'

We were soon entering the gates of Bradon Lodge and I unsnapped the top of my Gladstone bag and took out my Adams .450.

Port cast a glance at the weapon in my hand. 'Do you think as it's really dangerous then, sir?' he asked.

'You drive and I shall keep guard,' I answered. 'But let me know if you see anything unusual – anything at all.'

We reached the front of the house without incident and I took Port by the arm to stop him jumping down and reaching for my bag.

There was a sound of bolts being drawn and the front door opened a crack. Behind it I saw the face of the butler who had shown Holmes and me in on my previous visit.

'Will you come in, Doctor?' he called through the opening.

I shook my head. 'No. I shall guard Port while he stables the horse, then you must let us in very quickly from the stables.'

'Very well, sir.' He closed the door.

'Now, quickly,' I said to Port. 'Take us round to the stables!'

We rounded the side of the house and drew into a brick-paved stable yard. I sprang from the cart as soon as we were at a halt and made a rapid survey of the yard. 'Now,' I commanded. 'Get the dogcart put away and the horse seen to as fast as you can. I shall keep guard meanwhile.'

He backed the cart into a shed and unharnessed the horse, leading it into a stable. Once both were inside and I could see that there was no window or other entrance, I stood outside, pistol in hand, while he groomed the horse.

'Is it an escaped loony, sir?' he asked me as he worked. 'We ain't all that far from Broadmoor here, you know, sir.'

'No,' I said. 'An escaped mental patient would be a great deal easier to deal with.'

He emerged from the stable, wiping his hands on a piece of sacking. 'That's all done then, sir,' he reported.

'Good. Which of the doors in the back of the house is the best?' I asked, for I could see at least two.

'That one there goes straight into the kitchen.' He pointed at the right-hand one. 'But I ain't supposed to go into the kitchen in me yard boots.'

'Never mind,' I said. 'I don't imagine anyone will take you up on it. Now, you run to the kitchen door with the shotgun and knock hard. When you get there, keep your shotgun on the yard and I'll run across.'

He did as I bade him, standing with his back to the door when he reached it and banging with one fist, while his other moved the shotgun in a slow arc across the yard. I raced across with my bag and arrived just as the kitchen door opened. We tumbled in together, and the butler closed and bolted it behind us.

'Good afternoon, Dr Watson. Mrs Crosby is in the drawing room and has asked me to take you to her.' Saying which he led me through the crowd of puzzled and worried servants in the kitchen.

We found Mrs Crosby seated in the drawing room. She still wore full mourning, of course, but despite the alarms of the day her face was composed and I thought that I detected a determined tilt to her chin. 'Dr Watson.' She rose to greet me. 'How very good of you to respond so swiftly.'

'Not at all, madam. I only regret that Sherlock Holmes was not at Baker Street when your wire arrived. Nevertheless, I have left him your telegram and a note of my own actions, and I have no doubt we shall hear from him as soon as he is aware of the situation here.'

'I am only sorry to have bothered you,' she said. 'Inspector Hewitt here feels that, in fact, I have wasted your time as I have wasted his.' She spoke sharply and indicated with her hand a uniformed man who stood by the window.

He cleared his throat and stepped forward. 'I do not say that you have wasted my time, Mrs Crosby. We are always prepared to listen to the fears and problems of the public. I am sure that you were concerned for the safety of your little boys and I understand that, but in the end it all comes down to a story by two little lads who were playing – no doubt at cowboys and Indians. My officers have searched the garden and the grounds down to the stream, Mrs Crosby, and found no sign of any intruder at all, let alone an Indian savage.'

He turned to me. 'I'm sure it's very good of you to come all the way from London, Doctor, but I fear you are wasting your time.'

'Inspector,' I said, 'the prospect of some kind of savage being in this vicinity is a good deal more realistic than you seem to think. You cannot be unaware of the fate of Mrs Crosby's husband. Since that sad event, one of his employees has met a similar end in north Wales. I know it to be the view of my colleague, Mr Sherlock Holmes, that these outrages are the work of an Apache Indian. Were I you, I would not stand with my back to a window at present.'

He started and flung a nervous glance over his shoulder, then recovered himself and chuckled. 'Well, Doctor, I don't say as Mr Holmes hasn't had his results, and I am one who has enjoyed your accounts of them in the magazines, but when it comes down to practicalities, Doctor, there's not much chance of finding an Apache Indian in the woods of Hampshire.'

Mrs Crosby cast me a glance that showed her exasperation with the man.

'Then we must agree to differ,' I said curtly. 'You must do what you wish, or not do what you wish. I must take steps to ensure the safety of Mrs Crosby, her children and her servants.'

He picked up his cap. 'If that's your attitude, Doctor, there's really nothing more to be said. Mrs Crosby, on my way out I shall just take a last turn around the grounds, but I doubt I shall find any intruder. Good afternoon, madam. Good afternoon, Doctor.'

'I should tread very cautiously, if I were you,' I called after him as he left the room, but he ignored my comment.

When he had gone Mrs Crosby pressed a bell. 'You have dashed here from London and I have not even offered you tea, Doctor. Let us take some refreshment while I tell you exactly what has been happening here.'

Once we were seated and served she began her narrative: 'I think you know that I have two sons – Algernon and Augustus, fourteen and twelve respectively. They are sturdy, sensible boys, not given to silly imaginings, whatever the Inspector may say. My late husband raised them in his own mould, to have a spirit of curiosity and adventure, taking them out on his boat, teaching them to ride and to shoot, and so forth.' She looked steadily into my eyes and I remarked to myself once more that she was a very attractive woman. 'This morning Algy and Gus – that is what I call them – had gone out to play along the stream that borders our property at the bottom of the valley.'

She rose and walked to the window, beckoning me to follow. From the window we could see the rear lawns, the kitchen garden and a wide stretch of rough heathland, sloping gently down to the valley's bottom. To the right a mixed wood ran alongside the heath, following it down into the shallow valley and spreading into a wider forest on the opposite slope.

'You cannot see the stream,' she continued, as we returned to our seats, 'but it runs across the far end of our property and enters the wood on the right. Just before it flows into the wood it forms a little pool, quite attractive. It was near there that Gus and Algy were passing their time this morning. When they returned for their luncheon they told me that they had been watched at their play by a strange man.'

'What manner of man?' I asked.

'Well, at first they only thought there was someone there because they saw occasional movements and heard slight noises in the wood opposite them, but they had an old pair of my husband's field glasses with them and, at one point, they claim that the man was visible for an instant on the edge of the wood. Gus turned the glasses on him and he is very certain that what he saw there was a brown-skinned man whom he describes as "like a redskin – an Apache".'

'And you believe them?' I asked.

'My boys are old enough to know the difference between the inventions they employ in their games and reality, Dr Watson. They do not tell me lies. They thought the whole thing was a grand adventure, but I am not a fool, Doctor. I do not know how or why my husband came to die so horribly, or Teddy Danziger, but I can recall that the word "Apache" was on the list which I gave Mr Holmes and to which my husband seemed to attach great significance. For that reason I took the view that the man's appearance had some connection with my husband's death and I called the local police, and took steps to protect my sons and the servants. Now I hear you tell the Inspector that there is, indeed, an Apache Indian involved in this affair and I can only be glad that I acted promptly.'

'You have done very well and very wisely,' I told her, 'and it is a disgrace that Hewitt should not believe you. I am sure you are right.'

'What must we do, Doctor?' she asked.

'First I must speak to your boys and see if I can gather any further information from them; then we must take steps to ensure that these premises are absolutely secure and that a watch is set.'

Chapter Twenty-two

A Twilight Patrol

The Crosby boys were a credit to their parentage. Both tall for their ages, they had near identical faces, swept by thick fair hair and lit by eyes of bright blue. They tumbled into the drawing room side by side, immediately demanding of their mother that they be allowed to go out.

'It has stopped raining, Mama,' the younger boy pleaded. 'The sun has come out again.'

'You may not go out again until I say so, boys,' said their mother. 'This is Dr Watson, the associate of Mr Sherlock Holmes, the consulting detective. He has travelled here from London and we need your assistance.'

The announcement of my name quieted them for an instance. Then the younger boy nudged his brother in the ribs. 'Dr Watson!' he exclaimed.

The older boy stepped forward and extended his hand. 'I am Algernon Crosby, sir,' he said. 'Are you really the Dr Watson who writes for the *Strand* magazine?'

I nodded and Augustus came forward. 'I'm Augustus,' he said. 'Is Sherlock Holmes coming too?'

I smiled. 'I hope that he will join us as soon as he is

able. In the meantime, I need to know everything you can tell me about the man you saw this morning.'

They plumped down on to a couch and Augustus reached automatically for the plate of biscuits that had accompanied my tea.

'It was really Gussy who saw him,' said Algernon. 'You tell Dr Watson, Gussy.'

The younger boy began his narrative through a mouthful of biscuit crumbs. 'Well, we went out this morning looking for a hobby, because Algy said that he'd seen one yesterday by the pool.'

'A hobby?' I interrupted.

'It's a kind of migratory falcon, sir,' explained Algy. '*Falco subbuteo*, to give it the proper name, sir. I saw one yesterday by the pool. I knew it was a male hobby because of its red trousers, sir.'

'Anyway,' said Gussy, anxious to carry on with his story, 'I didn't believe him, because I'd never seen one around Bradon and I'm a far better birdwatcher than Algy. So we took father's old field glasses with us and we went down by the pool to see if there was one.'

'That's the pool where the stream flows into the woods?' I enquired.

Gussy nodded.

Algy said, 'They eat insects, sir, hobbies, so the pool attracts them, I think. It was by the pool I saw it yesterday, eating dragonflies, and thought it might have a nest in one of the tall trees along the edge of the woods.' He armed himself with another biscuit. 'So, after breakfast, Cook gave us some bread and cheese, and we went down by the pool to see,' he went on. 'You have to be very quiet while you're waiting for a bird and you listen for things. That's why we heard it, I suppose.'

'What did you hear?' I asked.

'Something or somebody creeping about in the woods across the other side of the pool,' his brother said. 'At first we thought it was an animal, but it began to sound more like a man.'

'What is the difference?'

'Well, sir, an animal is either very quiet or makes a lot of noise. Like the deer, sir – they either walk along the pathways in the wood and are very quiet, or they gallop through them and make a lot of bushes rustle – but this wasn't one thing or the other, sir. It sounded like some-one who was trying not to make a noise, but every now and then he did.'

'And what did you think?' I asked.

'We didn't think much about it,' said Gus. 'We were concentrating on whether there was a hobby coming, so we didn't pay much attention.'

'I thought it might be a poacher,' said Algy, 'but he wasn't on our side of the stream, so I didn't worry about it.'

'Then it sounded as though he had crossed over,' said Gus, 'because we heard the same little noises coming from this side, where the edge of the woods is.'

'I was going to shout and tell him that it was private land,' said Algy, 'and I was looking to see if I could see anyone on the edge of the wood, and that's when I saw the hobby. It was perched on a tree, so I pointed it out to Gussy.'

'I had the field glasses,' said Gus, 'so I looked where Algy pointed and just as looked I saw a man pop his head out of the bushes at the edge of the wood. It was very lucky, he was right in my glasses.'

'I only caught a glimpse of him, then he went back into the bushes,' said Algy, 'but Gus says he saw him clearly.'

'Well, I saw his face clearly,' the younger boy amended.

'And what did he look like?' I asked.

'I think he was short for a man, but he might have been bending. He had a very brown face and bright black eyes. His hair was all down around his shoulders and he had a band tied round his forehead, and there was a string round his neck with some things tied on it.'

'And what did you think he was?' I enquired.

'I didn't know what he was, at first. He wasn't the same kind of brown as the Indians who sell carpets in Winchester, and he wasn't the same as the Lascars and negroes at Southampton, but I knew I'd seen something like him before. Then I thought and I remembered that there are pictures like him in the *Bumper Redskin Book* that Father gave me. So I was sure he was an Apache.'

'Did he see you two?'

'No, sir. Father taught us to lie well under the brush when using the glasses so that the lenses wouldn't reflect the sunlight and birds wouldn't be frightened. Do you think he was an Apache, sir?' Algy wanted to know. 'What was he doing here?'

'I'm certain that he is an Apache,' I told him, 'and his presence here means no good. That is why your mother called the police and has taken steps to protect the house.'

'But the Inspector didn't believe Gussy.' Algy sounded very affronted. 'Gussy's a bit of a donkey sometimes, but he wouldn't tell lies about something like that.'

'No, sir, I wouldn't,' the younger boy added.

'Well, I believe you,' I said. 'And I know this man is very dangerous, so you must both do exactly what your mother tells you.'

'Take the field glasses up to the nursery,' Mrs Crosby told them. 'While it is light you can keep a watch from the rear window.'

They scampered away, apparently unaffected by the fear that their news had spread through the house.

'You do believe Gussy, Dr Watson?' said Mrs Crosby.

'Absolutely. As I told Inspector Hewitt, Sherlock Holmes is convinced that your husband's death was the work of an Apache and I have heard descriptions of such a man as your sons saw. It is imperative that this house is defended as strongly as possible.'

'I have already had all ground-floor windows closed and locked, and all doors locked and bolted,' she confirmed.

'We must consider the second storey,' I said. 'This man can climb like a cat.'

Together we traversed every inch of the house, ensuring that each window was securely catched and shuttered where light was not necessary. At windows where there was a wide view of the surrounding ground I placed the grooms and gardeners, each with a handbell and a firearm.

I became aware that there was likely to be no threat until after dark. The house stood among lawns and flowerbeds at the front, with more lawns and the kitchen garden at the rear. There was no cover of any significance in any direction within many yards and anyone making an approach, however stealthy, could readily be seen from an upstairs window. I believed that our opponent was likely to be concealed in the woods, awaiting the dark so that he could approach the house unseen. Briefly I weighed the advisability of taking the armed staff into the woods and beating through them, in the hope of flushing him out, but I feared that he would take the opportunity to use his silent arrows and knives against them to disastrous effect.

Nevertheless I did not intend that we should wait supinely until he launched himself against us. As soon as the sun reached the horizon, I took my Adams .450 and my stick, and had the butler let me out from a side door. I cast across the front of the house at first, but the front lawns and drive were undisturbed. Going across to where the woods joined the garden, I began to move down alongside the edge of the wood, stepping as stealthily as I might and intending, if necessary, to follow the flank of the trees all the way down to the stream. There was still ample light for me to peer a fair distance into the wood as I went along but by the time I had paralleled the side of the house and the stable block at the rear I had detected no indication of anyone in the trees.

Emerging behind the building, I paused to scan the landscape. To my left the heathland attached to the gardens was still well lit by the dying sun. It was all small scrub, heather and moss, with no real cover anywhere in its expanse. I continued to move parallel to the wood, still peering in between the trunks.

I was well down towards the stream and had heard no untoward sound nor seen any indication of disturbance or movement when I spotted something dark lying on the ground ahead of me. It was largely concealed by a slight hummock, but its darkness seemed unnatural and I thought caught the glint of metal. At first I believed that it was the Indian, pressed to the ground for concealment, but then I realised that he would have no need to do so in close proximity to the wood. I could not imagine what it might be, so I approached with extra caution.

As I topped the slight rise that had concealed it, I saw at once that it was Inspector Hewitt. It took but a moment to determine that he was dead, for one of the Apache's characteristic arrows had taken him from behind, pierced the heart and emerged partly at the front. I was sorry for the Inspector's death, albeit brought on by his own folly, but it occurred to me rapidly that this might be a blessing in disguise. Nothing stirs the police to activity like the murder of one of their own. I had only to return to the house and telephone my news to Southampton to have Bradon Lodge and its environs swarming with police officers in a trice.

It had grown perceptibly darker as I stooped over the unfortunate Inspector's body, so I abandoned my patrol and sprang away across the heathland, making for the rear of the house. I had not gone ten yards when something unseen entangled my running feet and I fell heavily, not on to the ground, but into a pit of some kind. My head struck its edge a ringing blow and darkness swallowed me.

Chapter Twenty-three

The Dragon Pit

How long I lay there I cannot tell. When at last I began to recover my senses I found that I was in what seemed to be a disused gravel pit and above its edges was almost total darkness. I tried to move, but found my head still ached from the blow that had robbed me of consciousness and I could put no weight on my right leg. As well as I might in the almost pitch darkness I felt myself all over. I was bruised in a number of places, though not seriously, and my hands and face were abraded by contact with the rough sides of the pit. A lump as large as a pigeon's egg was evident on my head, but I did not seem to be concussed. I had feared that my right leg might be broken, but my manual examination confirmed that I had merely sprained the ankle.

Having taken stock of my injuries, I looked next to my surroundings. The pit was some ten feet deep and about twenty feet across. It had evidently not been used for some time, for grass and moss had accumulated on its sides, but the steepness of those sides and my enfeebled right ankle made it unlikely that I would be able to clamber out. I had a suspicion that whatever had tripped me as I ran away from Inspector Hewitt's corpse was a deliberate device of some kind – most probably a tripwire – and that our Apache foe had lured me into a trap. Not knowing how long I had lain in the pit, I could not know how long it might be before he returned to administer the *coup de grâce*. I felt in my pockets for my pistol, but could not find it.

Cautiously, I felt around the bottom of the pit, but still could not locate my weapon. Eventually I took a box of Vestas from my pocket and struck one, quickly scanning my surroundings in the light of the match. There was no sign of my Adams anywhere and I recalled that I had held it in my hand while I examined the Inspector's body and when I ran for assistance, It would have flown from my hand when I tumbled and most probably lay somewhere above me and beyond my reach. I was disabled and helpless, entirely at the mercy of our savage adversary if he chose to return.

I cast about the pit again, seeking anything which I might use as a weapon, though the exercise was more to stiffen my morale than for any other purpose. I was too well aware that the Apache had only to stand at the pit's edge and deploy his deadly arrows or knives and I would have no defence. I gathered near to me a pile of the largest stones I could find on the pit's bottom, set my back firmly against the side of the excavation and prepared to sell my life as dearly as circumstances permitted.

Time passed and I began to perceive a slight lightening of the sky above. Overcast still made the stars invisible, but a weak moon must have risen and shed a faint light, which made it easier to see the rim of my prison. I longed to smoke a cigarette, but dared not take the risk. I imagined that the Indian's olfactory senses would be highly sensitive and, if he was not aware of my presence in the pit, I had no intention of signalling it by the smell of tobacco smoke.

I must have lain there for some four hours before there was any development. The night had turned chilly and the dew was down, so that I became cold, damp and cramped. From time to time I was forced to shift my position and carry out sitting exercises, both to prevent cramp setting in too severely and to warm myself. It was during one of these sessions that I thought I heard sounds apart from the slight noise of my own movements. I lay still and listened as keenly as I might. From somewhere close to the edge of the pit I thought that I could hear a soft swishing sound, as though something fairly large was moving rhythmically through the low growth on the heath above. I did not know whether I had heard the sound of some nocturnal animal going its rounds or whether the Apache was approaching my prison, but I grasped a stone in each hand and peered around me at the pit's perimeter.

Suddenly something dark interrupted the skyline on the edge of the pit opposite me. Without hesitation I flung a stone as hard and as accurately as I could in that direction. I did not hit it, but its startled yelp as it leapt away made me certain that I had merely been visited by a fox.

I fell to wondering what the reaction of Mrs Crosby must be to my disappearance. I felt certain that one or another of the watchers I had set at the upper windows would have seen my progress along the margin of the woods and maybe even my fall into the pit. Surely by now Mrs Crosby would have telephoned the police and informed them of my disappearance, and it could not be long before a search party swept the heathland and found me. The prospect heartened me and I began fervently to hope that relief would arrive before I was forced to try conclusions with the Apache.

It may have been that another hour had passed when I heard the faint swishing sound again. It crossed my mind that, when the fox visited me, I had been wrong to cast a stone. Had it been our enemy he would, by my action, have realised that I was both awake and aggressive. It might be better to feign sleep or unconsciousness until he was about to attack me and then do my best with my limited armament. With this in mind I lay silent, listening to the faint sound of movement passing almost right around the pit until it ceased at a point nearly opposite me. I gripped my stone and waited.

So slowly as to be almost imperceptible at first, something dark raised itself against my limited skyline. Although I could not see his features, I believed it to be the enemy's head. He was not yet in a position to loose an arrow or a knife, and I waited, straining my eyes in the gloom for the first sign of any arm movement that might signal an attack. To my surprise, none came. Instead the head withdrew and I heard further slight sounds, which I was not able to interpret. Then the head appeared again and a blood-curdlingly guttural chuckle sounded softly, before the Apache sprang to his feet and disappeared.

I was at a loss to understand his action, until I heard faint noises from within the pit itself. With a horrible leap of understanding I realised the cause of that sinister chuckle. He had released a rattlesnake, or maybe more than one, into my prison.

I have always considered myself to be a man of reasonably firm nerve, as a doctor must be, but if ever my nerve was on the point of cracking it was then. I cannot recollect without strong emotion the cold horror that flooded my being when I thought that I was sharing that black hole with a deadly reptile.

Steadying myself, I recalled that snakes are usually afraid of mankind and that, if I could see it, I might stand a chance of killing or disabling it with a stone. Taking my matches from my pocket I struck one and held it high in an attempt to locate my adversary. If I had been horrified at the thought of a rattlesnake, my senses reeled at the sight revealed by the flare of my match. Crawling steadily down the side of the pit opposite were three creatures of a kind I had never seen before, even in my worst nightmares. They were not snakes, but monstrous lizards, each some two feet long or more. Their expressionless saurian eyes glinted in the flame's light, while their tongues flicked like a snake's from their mouths. Their long, rounded bodies were blotched with light and dark patterns and bands, and they moved on short legs. While I could not recall the proper name for these hideous creatures, I remembered that Arizona made a home to the world's only poisonous lizard and I knew instinctively that this was what had been unleashed against me.

I would a thousand times rather have died a clean and instant death like that of the Inspector, taken by one straight shot to the heart, than face these primaeval brutes in the darkness, waiting until they reached the pit's floor and commenced their attack upon me. I levered myself upright and braced myself against the side, waiting to defend myself, but I knew that I could not climb beyond their reach and that, there being three of them, my prospects of disabling or killing all three with stones in the dark were virtually non-existent.

The thought of darkness made me recollect that I had one slender advantage, for as long as it lasted. When I had struck my match all three of the creatures had flinched away from its light. If they were by nature nocturnal, fire and light were weapons I could use against them. Quickly I scrabbled together a heap of dried grass and twigs from the pit's floor, adding to them some unpaid bills and unanswered correspondence from my coat pocket, before setting a match to the pile. As my match caught the paper and flame illuminated the pit, I saw all three lizards draw back, hissing, and remain motionless A small surge of hope flickered in me. Not only had I startled the creatures into a standstill, if there were any search for me the fire's light would draw a rescue party.

The first flare of the burning papers dwindled and the twigs and grass were slow to catch fire, so that the flames lowered, encouraging the monsters opposite to begin a slow flanking approach, two to one side and one to the other. I could not create a complete barrier of flame between them and myself and realised that, eventually, they would find their way around the fire. I slipped off my coat and removed my shirt, flinging it on to my little fire to increase the size of the flames. The result was satisfactory, bringing them to a hissing halt once again. With my jacket I fanned the fire, brightening the flames and sending smoke towards the serpents, an effect which they evidently disliked, for they withdrew slightly.

For a short time I actually believed that I might have mastered the situation. Indeed, had I possessed a branch of sufficient length, I could have lighted it and driven my obscene attackers out of the pit, but I was tied to my static fire. All too soon, it began to dwindle again and the lizards, emboldened, began their stealthy flanking crawl again. In desperation I started to consider adding my trousers to the conflagration and had, in fact, begun to unfasten my braces when a quiet voice spoke from above.

'Watson,' said the familiar tones of Sherlock Holmes, 'stir up the fire as much as you can and stand back against the side of the hole.'

There have been numerous occasions in my life when I have given heartfelt thanks for the intervention of my friend, but few when the sound of his voice and the knowledge of his presence brought me such relief as on that night in Hampshire. I wasted no time in doing his bidding, stirring up the remaining elements of the fire to as bright a glow as possible, then pressing back against the pit's wall.

As the lizards flinched away from the renewed flame

a pistol barked four times from somewhere above me, and each of them writhed in its death agonies. A loop of rope slid down beside me and Holmes instructed me: 'Watson, put your good foot in the loop and hold on.' Within seconds I had been drawn up and lay sprawled in the heather, panting with relief more than exertion.

Holmes bent over me with a lantern and examined my pale and smoke-smeared face. 'Are you all right, Watson?' he asked, with an emphasis of concern that warmed my heart.

'Nothing worse that a bruised head and a sprained ankle,' I managed to gasp. 'That was a nice piece of shooting, Holmes.'

'I should have managed it with three shots,' he demurred.

I recalled the dead Inspector. 'Holmes,' I said, 'Inspector Hewitt . . .'

But he forestalled me: 'We have found him. You may credit your rescue to Algy and Gus Crosby, who watched you from the nursery window. I arrived just after dark and they were like leashed bloodhounds. They knew you had disappeared somewhere over here, but their mother – very wisely – refused to allow anyone to leave the house until the police arrived. They, of course, took a deal of convincing, but the body of their Inspector seems to have roused them to their task.'

With my friend's assistance I clambered to my feet. Around us I could see the dark shapes of policemen with lanterns, combing the heath and moving towards the black bulk of the woods, but cold and reaction were working on me, and I had no interest in awaiting the result of their search.

'You are shivering, Watson,' said Holmes. Sliding out of his coat, he draped it about my shoulders. 'Let us leave them to their tasks and get you back to the house,' he added.

'What', I demanded, as we made our way slowly

towards the building, 'were those horrifying creatures in the pit?'

'You surprise me, Watson. I should have thought that your endless reading of novels of cowboy adventures might have made you familiar with *heloderma suspectum*, more commonly known as the Gila monster. They have particularly unpleasant teeth and their bite is fatal.'

'But where on earth would he have acquired them?' I asked. 'Surely you cannot buy those things in the East End?'

'I doubt', said Holmes, 'whether Wan Fat keeps them, though I shall enquire, but since our Apache almost certainly came to Britain by working his passage, he most probably brought them with him. As Wan Fat told us, sailors sell him all manner of creatures and he would have had little difficulty in shipping them in a box as pets he intended to sell in London'.

It was well into the following afternoon when I woke in a bed at Bradon Lodge to find my meal brought to me, not by the servants, but by Algy and Gus who had, apparently, been chafing all day to hear from my own lips the story of my misadventures. As I told them what had happened I found it hard to believe that I was really lying in a comfortable bed with good food spread before me, so convinced had I been a few hours before that I was likely to end my life in that black pit of serpents.

When I had eaten Holmes arrived. 'If you are able to travel tomorrow, Watson, I am arranging a small conference at Baker Street. I think it is high time that we carried the war into the enemy's camp. By the way,' he added, 'I wired Wan Fat to see if he stocked Gila monsters. His reply is interesting.' He passed me the telegram. It said:

GILA MONSTERS RARE AND VENOMOUS STOP HAVE NEVER BOUGHT OR SOLD ONE STOP YOU TELL HOW MANY YOU WANT I GET THEM FOR YOU

Chapter Twenty-four

Reconnaissance and Strategy

Had it rested with the Crosby boys as to when I left their home I should be there still, propped up in bed and retailing to them narratives of experiences that I had shared with Sherlock Holmes, but my ankle was fit for use in a day, and Holmes and I were soon on our way to London. Remembering the unfortunate Inspector Hewitt's attitude when first I arrived at Bradon Lodge, I was pleased to note as we left that a strong police presence was being maintained in and around the house.

It occurred to me, on our way home, to ask Holmes if he was sure that the killer had withdrawn once more to London, for the Hampshire police had been unable to find him.

'They might have saved themselves a deal of effort if they had done as I did,' he remarked. 'It was evident to me that the man had not walked from London dragging his unpleasant pets behind him – he must have used the train. While you were recovering, I took the opportunity of a word with the stationmaster, who confirmed my suspicion. A man of the right description left Bradon by the first workman's train yesterday morning. The stationmaster thought him a gypsy.'

'So we must confront him in London,' I said. 'When I came down here I had hoped that we might end it here.'

'It was a possibility,' agreed Holmes. 'Your measures to protect Bradon Lodge were excellent and, had I arrived a little sooner and had you not fallen into his trap . . .'

'It was a trap?' I interrupted.

'Oh, indeed, Watson. A wire had been stretched across the direct path from Hewitt's body to the house, so that it would trip anyone into the gravel pit.'

'And I stumbled into it,' I remarked bitterly.

'You should not blame yourself, Watson. As it is, our encounter with him in Hampshire has confirmed my view that, away from his own territory, he will make mistakes.'

'He has made none so far,' I contradicted.

'He has twice failed to kill each of us,' said Holmes, 'and he failed to find the map at Graby's, but on the heath at Bradon Lodge he made another mistake.'

'What was that?' I asked.

Holmes smiled. 'For all his care to swaddle his boots with grass, he is a man of the desert and the mountains. He is not used to our low-growing grass and heather, sodden with dew. When I emerged from the house to search for you, I had a dark lantern which I dared not use and only a general idea of where you had fallen. I should not have worried, for even the faint moonlight available showed me our friend's error – a wide black trail through the heather and grass, where he had brushed away the dew. London is even more foreign to him, Watson, and he will make greater mistakes.'

When I rose the next morning my ankle was completely recovered, but Holmes surprised me by insisting that I spend the day in rest. 'Tomorrow night, Watson,

I expect you to need that ankle.' But he would explain no more of his intentions. He did, however, tell me that he had invited Lestrade and Major Braithwaite to dine with us that evening.

I was, therefore, startled when, in the late afternoon, he announced that he was going out on what he called 'a reconnaissance'.

'Holmes!' I complained. 'You have invited guests!'

'Events may force me to be a little late.'

'Lestrade and the Major may put up with it,' I said, 'but Mrs Hudson will be furious.'

'Mrs Hudson has become very good over the years at not being furious with me,' he stated. 'Besides, since it is a warm evening, I have suggested a cold repast so as to cause the least disruption. As to Lestrade and the Major – Lestrade knows me of old and I am sure that you will stand deputy for me with the Major.' With which he was gone.

In due course our guests arrived and I found myself at the distinct disadvantage of having no smallest idea of my friend's intentions. Mrs Hudson's cold service was fully suited to the warm evening and we enjoyed our food but, once we had got past the ordinary civilities, it became evident that we were all agog to know why Holmes had called us together.

The dinner cleared, pipes and cigarettes lighted, we sat silent around a decanter of port, listening to the occasional hansom rattle through the street and the fainter, but more continuous clatter of the Marylebone Road, borne to us through the open windows.

Lestrade had gone so far as to look at his watch twice and I was silently cursing Holmes when, at last, we heard his footfall on the stairs. He strode into the room with a broad smile upon his features. 'Major Braithwaite, Lestrade,' so glad that you were both available. If you will bear with me while I change, I have, I believe, good news.'

In his absence I rang for Mrs Hudson to serve Holmes's food and soon he was at the table, eating voraciously and talking almost without interruption.

'The problem', he explained, 'has always been to establish where abouts in London the Apache had made his citadel. Now, we had the good fortune that Wan Fat pointed us in the right direction, though I should have sought him in the dock area as being the region in which his presence would cause the least remark, but that led me only to his place of work. As I might have expected, even when I worked alongside him on the quaysides he told me nothing of himself, being, it seems, a man who believes that one word is usually sufficient. As a result I was forced to follow him home – or rather to make the attempt.'

Major Braithwaite laughed. 'I am not surprised that you failed, Mr Holmes, even in London.'

'Oh, but I succeeded in the end. On the first few occasions he lost me completely, but on three occasions I tracked him to the same area. Always I lost him in the vicinity of Brewers Lane.'

'Brewers Lane?' I said, some recollection stirring at the back of my mind.

'Indeed. The selfsame location from which Mr Graby acquired his illicit supply of Admiralty marine paint. Now, it was my efforts on the docks that brought me into contact with those who knew about Graby's dishonest habits and whence his goods came, so I had no occasion to visit Brewers Lane, but when Graby mentioned the damaged warehouse it occurred to me that some such place might form a very useful hideout for our Indian assassin, so I have examined it with some care.'

With the back of his knife he began to sketch a diagram on the tablecloth. 'The burned-out warehouse stands second along Brewers Lane from the river front. Next to it – here – is the warehouse which Graby looted.

That was not nearly so badly damaged. Those old warehouses were mostly built with huge, open undercrofts as a ground floor. That is the area to which the fire spread, destroying the goods there and burning out the bottom of the stairs at front and rear, and the lower level of the internal hoist. That is why it has proved difficult to remove the items stored above. Our Apache, however, is a man of extreme agility, as we have learned. It occurred to me that anyone who could reach the second floor would have four floors of the warehouse to himself and a position that was remarkably easy to defend, similar, in many respects, to the mountain caves of his homeland.'

Braithwaite nodded thoughtfully. 'That would make a deal of sense,' he agreed. 'A high place that's inaccessible, except to one man at a time. That sounds like the sort of place he'd choose.'

'But are you sure he is there, Mr Holmes?' asked Lestrade.

'This afternoon it was a reasonable theory,' said Holmes. 'This evening I am moderately certain that I am right. That was why I had to leave you to dine without me.'

'But surely he was back there this evening?' I protested.

'Exactly, Watson, and there was a safe and simple method of determining his presence. Since he knows his stronghold to be almost unassailable, he does not need to live in darkness. I have passed a part of this evening sitting in a boat on the river, watching Bourton's Warehouse for a sign of life – a light, in fact. I have seen it, a candle flame moving about on the third floor. He is there, gentlemen, and now that we know where he is, we can take him.' He looked around him like a conjurer presenting a successful trick.

I fear that he was not met with the enthusiasm that he expected.

'Easier said than done,' mumbled Lestrade. 'You yourself called it "almost unassailable".'

'Remember the "almost", Lestrade,' said Holmes, unabashed. 'It would certainly not be possible to attack from the ground floor, but there lies our advantage.'

'We might collect a large body of constables and take the undercroft by storm,' mused Lestrade.

'And he would pick them off, one by one, as they tried to get higher,' said the Major. 'I think I see the direction you're going in, Mr Holmes. You believe that he only expects attack from below . . .'

'Precisely, Major,' Holmes interrupted him. 'So he will not expect and will not have provided for an attack from above.'

'But how can you get above him?' Lestrade wondered.

'First,' said Holmes, 'I draw your attention to my diagram. These lines at the top indicate the Thames. The square box immediately below is Bourton's Warehouse. The box below that is the burned-out warehouse. Along the right-hand side of the two warehouses runs Brewers Lane, which extends to the river bank and then turns right along the river. Across the front of the burned building – here at the bottom – is Smithy Street. To the left of both buildings is a large yard, partly filled with old barrels and crates.'

We all examined Holmes's markings on the table-cloth.

'You can see', he went on, 'that our friend's fortress is immediately adjacent to the river on one side, so no approach from that side can be made without difficulty. On the opposite side the building is blocked by its burned-out neighbour. That leaves us Brewers Lane or the rear yard as ways of access.'

'But surely', objected Lestrade, 'the windows are barred on both sides.'

'So they are,' Holmes agreed. 'I had considered the

use of a screw jack, but it would take too much time and produce too much noise.'

'Then how can we gain access?' I asked.

'On Brewers Lane, and in the rear yard, are chain hoists,' said Holmes. 'I believe that, if Lestrade's force of constables holds the ground, sealing the perimeter of the premises, and a couple of River Police steam launches take the waterside, a small body of men may be swiftly hoisted to the roof via the two chain hoists.'

Braithwaite smiled slowly. 'It sounds a good plan, Mr Holmes, but you admit you can only raise a small body of men by the hoists. They will need to be pretty determined characters, so as to overwhelm him quickly, otherwise you'll have a desperate battle inside the warehouse in the dark – the kind of situation an Apache loves.'

'I imagine so and for that reason I shall go up by the rear hoist, from the yard, accompanied by . . .'

'Me,' I interrupted, for there was no way that I intended to let Holmes confront the Indian without my assistance.

He nodded his head. 'With Watson,' he finished. 'Who else?'

'Then I should go up on the front hoist,' said Lestrade and Holmes nodded again. 'Whom will you have with you?' he asked the little detective.

Before Lestrade could open his mouth, Major Braithwaite intervened: 'Just hold on! I appreciate that I'm a foreigner, but I have a good claim to be part of this operation of yours.'

'You are a citizen of the United States,' said Lestrade in a shocked tone. 'You cannot be permitted to intervene in the operations of the Metropolitan Police.'

'Lieutenant,' began Braithwaite, pronouncing the word in the American fashion.

'Inspector if you please, Major,' said the little detective

huffily. 'They have lieutenants [emphasising the English pronunciation] in Scotland, I believe.'

Braithwaite laughed aloud. 'Very well, Inspector, I apologise, but we also have lieutenants of detectives in America.'

'Is that a fact?' asked Lestrade, as though the idea was totally unfamiliar to him.

'Gentlemen,' said Holmes, 'we are all supposed to be on the same side here. What did you wish to say, Major?'

'I was about to remark that you are a freelance, a private agent, a consulting detective, and you it was who tracked the Apache to his lair, not the official police. So, Inspector, if Mr Holmes says there are good reasons why I shouldn't take part, then I'll listen to them, but I have the best qualifications out of all of us – I have spent years trailing and fighting Apache Indians. Which of you can say the same?' He gazed about the table pugnaciously.

Holmes smiled. 'A powerful argument, Major, and one that I have no intention of denying. So long as you are aware of the very real dangers of what I propose – and I suspect you realise them more accurately than any of us – I see no reason why you should not join us.'

Braithwaite relaxed and Lestrade said nothing.

'What about armament?' I asked.

'We know', said Holmes, 'that our prey is a crack shot with a bow and arrow, and a deadly knife thrower. He has not used firearms, so far as we know, but that does not mean that he does not have them. I shall carry a pistol. Watson, I imagine, will bring his Adams. What about you, Lestrade?'

'I shall draw a weapon,' he replied. 'I shall also see that some of the uniformed lads are armed.'

'It would be as well,' Holmes agreed. 'Major, what about you?'

Major Braithwaite dropped a silver-mounted Derringer on the table, though from where it appeared I had no idea. 'I had thought that I was coming to a law-abiding city.' He grinned. 'So that's the extent of my armament.'

'Oh, I'm sure we can find you more than that,' said Holmes.

'I've been thinking about these here hoists,' Lestrade mused. 'They make a devil of a noise, you know. He can't fail to hear them working, so he'll be ready for us.'

Holmes shook his head. 'I doubt it,' he said. 'I shall take a leaf out of Mr Handel's book and distract him when the time comes.'

Chapter Twenty-five

By Land and by Water

It was not much later when our meeting ended, and Lestrade and the American took themselves off. I was soon in my bed and I believe that Holmes was not long after me in retiring.

He was already gone when I arose next day, but he returned at teatime, rubbing his hands with pleasure, and swallowed a hearty meal. He said nothing of the intended operation and I merely awaited his instructions.

It was growing dark when he had me check our pistols, including an extra one for Major Braithwaite, and we summoned a four-wheeler. By the time we had collected the Major from his hotel and Lestrade from Scotland Yard it was fully dark as we made our way through the flare-lit Commercial Road, already astir with painted women and their potential customers.

At the corner of Brewers Lane we paused, while Holmes pointed out the battleground: 'Here, nearest to us, is the burned-out warehouse – that great grey building. Its interior is completely destroyed. Beyond it there – towards the river – is Bourton's Warehouse. If Lestrade's men can hold the perimeter and we can surprise him from above, then our action will take place between the upper and second storeys of that building.'

He told our cabby to take us into the darkened yard at the rear of the two warehouses. As soon as we stepped from our vehicle I became aware of the silent presence of a large body of uniformed police officers drawn up in the yard, their dark clothes and helmets almost melting into the summer night and only patches of pale faces beneath their headgear revealing their whereabouts.

'Your men are admirably quiet,' Holmes told Lestrade. 'Are the River Police in position?'

'There are two launches with electric searchlights, as you requested, Mr Holmes. They will show no light until you signal them.'

'Very good,' Holmes nodded. 'I suggest that you now tell your men to spread silently around the entire ground level of Bourton's building, watching and stopping every possible exit. Nothing must emerge until I do. In the meantime, take Major Braithwaite round into Brewers Lane. The chain hoist has been lowered to ground level and I myself have oiled it today. When I signal, have your men lift the two of you, as swiftly as possible, to the rooftop. Watson and I will join you from this side.'

'What about the rattle of the hoists?' asked Lestrade.

'Have no fear,' replied Holmes. 'That has been taken care of.'

He picked up the Gladstone bag which he had brought with him and strode towards the wall of the warehouse, beckoning me to follow. At the foot of the wall stood a small platform, attached by chains to the main chain of the hoist, which stretched away above us into the darkness. We mounted the platform and took a firm grip of an iron bar that looped above us.

'How will you signal Lestrade?' I asked.

'With this,' said Holmes and drew from his coat pocket a marine signal pistol. Pointing it into the air he pulled the trigger, unleashing a shell, which soared over the warehouse and burst in a bright star of green light. Immediately a team of Lestrade's constables set to work to raise us and the hoist's platform left the ground with a jerk.

Occupied as I was with keeping my balance, I was nevertheless aware of two other effects that had begun with Holmes's signal. From somewhere beneath us came a rhythmic pounding and rattling of chains, while out on the river a cascade of bright lights burst around a chain of small boats moored in the middle of the stream. Rockets were fired from them, and flares of all colours lit the night and reflected on the Thames's dark waters.

'What on earth is going on, Holmes?' I gasped.

'Lestrade was concerned about the noise of our ascent,' Holmes smiled. 'I have paid the engineman at Bevington's Yard there to run his steam winch and drag a bundle of chains up and down their launching ramp. Meanwhile, in order to distract our quarry, I invited my Baker Street Irregulars to stage a small firework display on the river, to which they very readily agreed.'

I was sure that Holmes's corps of ragged street arabs were having the time of their young lives out on the river, but I was not sure that the device would work. 'Won't he realise that something unusual is afoot?' I said, the breeze almost whipping away my words.

'Oh, indubitably,' Holmes agreed, 'but he will be used to Mexican religious ceremonies with fireworks and he will not know that we do not celebrate so often or in the same fashion. You may depend upon it – he will be at the window, watching the fireworks.'

The team below worked hard at the hoist and we continued to lift into the air. Now that we were above most of the surrounding buildings the breeze was stronger, threatening to snatch our caps from our heads and carrying away the smell of the river in summer and the workshops that clustered about the docks. To the east, past Blackwall, the river and the city were in darkness, but in the other direction the last faint embers of sunset smouldered behind the buildings.

At last we came to the head of the hoist. Sherlock Holmes sprang effortlessly on to the warehouse roof, reaching out to steady the hoist as I joined him. As my eyes grew accustomed to the gloom on the building's top I saw that Lestrade and Major Braithwaite were scrambling on to the far side.

Holmes strode silently across the flat roof, though noise would have mattered little for the steam winch could be heard pounding and rattling away beneath us, and the cacophony of fireworks still echoed from the river.

Lestrade and his companion joined us where Holmes knelt beside a dusty skylight. Opening his bag, my friend drew out a canister of some black substance and, with a twist of rag, daubed it generously all over a pane of the skylight. Reaching again into the bag he extracted a folded piece of canvas and spread it on the smeared pane. He ran a glass cutter swiftly and firmly around the edges of the canvas, then took hold of a wrinkle in the material and delivered a sharp knock at the edge of the pane with his pistol's butt. The weakened glass came free of its frame, and Holmes lifted it silently and effortlessly away from the skylight, laying it flat on the roof.

'You would have made a slick second-storey man,' murmured Braithwaite.

'In the practice of my singular profession I have found it necessary to acquire certain skills,' acknowledged Holmes. 'Lestrade, you're the smallest. Would you care to have the honour?' He had taken a rope from his bag and now lowered it through the missing pane into the warehouse, bracing it against his back.

Lestrade stepped forward, slid into the hole in the skylight and, grasping the rope with both hands, lowered himself into the pitch-black depths beneath. One by one we followed him until we stood, in darkness so complete that we could barely see each other, below the violated window.

'Where is the Apache, Mr Holmes?' Braithwaite whispered.

'Unless I miss my guess,' said Holmes, 'he will be on the floor below us, somewhere near the windows that look out on to the river.'

The floor on which we stood was very dark, lit occasionally by the distant flare of fireworks through the stained and dusty window-panes, and the skylight by which we had entered, but it was impossible to see any detail. From under his coat Holmes drew a dark lantern, opening its slide by the tiniest fraction and letting the slender beam of light swing across the warehouse floor around us. Eventually it paused on the stairhead.

'This way, gentlemen,' he invited, 'and no unnecessary sound.' He closed the lantern and made away towards the stairs, all of us following after him. This floor of the warehouse was largely empty and open space stretched between us and the stairhead. Had it not been, I doubt if I could have found my way noiselessly across the floor, but we were soon gathered by the stairs.

Holmes opened the lantern once more and flicked its beam quickly into the stairwell. We caught a glimpse of sturdy, worn timber treads and a rope banister at both sides. Holmes first, we began a slow, cautious and silent descent on to the floor below.

If the warehouse floors were dark, the stairwell was absolutely pitch-black. Treading cautiously, as Holmes had long taught me, placing each foot softly but firmly on the outer ends of the treads, so as to avoid any unnecessary creaking of the old timbers, I followed my invisible friend down the steps, at every moment afraid that I would step too far in the inky dark, bump into Holmes and precipitate both of us into a roll down the remaining stairs. Equally, I feared to linger too long on any step lest Braithwaite, who was immediately behind me, should stumble into me. With my Adams in my right hand, I managed to guide myself by keeping an almost continuous contact with the rope banister on my left.

Miraculously, we all reached the bottom of the stairs without mishap and with no sound that even the sharpest ear would have heard against the distant throbbing and rattling of the steam winch and the explosions on the river.

At the stairs' foot Holmes stepped quietly on to the warehouse floor and brought me to a halt beside him with a gesture. Blinded by the pitch-dark stairwell, my eyes reacted more quickly to the faint light now available to us. I soon saw that we had emerged near to the blind side of the warehouse – that is, the side that abutted on the burned-out building. A wide floor, stacked with rows and heaps of barrels, tea chests, bales and boxes, stretched away to our left, where a row of arched windows appeared, their grimy panes lit by faint moonlight and occasional bursts of pale colour as another flare burst over the river. In one corner of the furthest window I saw a dark mass on the windowsill and, as I strained to distinguish the details, the shape moved slightly. I knew then that Holmes had been right and that his firework display had drawn our quarry to the riverside windows.

As we stood in silence, Holmes explained by gestures what he required. He pointed where four alleyways led between the rows of merchandise in the direction of the windows and indicated that he wished us to take one each. Covered by the continuing barrage from the river, we slunk noiselessly across the floor until each was in his appointed place, then began a silent movement towards the windows.

We had traversed almost half the length of the walkways when disaster struck. Holmes was in the passage to my left and Braithwaite to my right. From the far right passageway I heard a small, sharp sound, like the cracking of something thin and brittle. I knew at once that Lestrade had stepped upon something and given us away.

A guttural exclamation broke from the dark shape at the windows. Holmes, Braithwaite and I fired simultaneously, but in a flash the figure disappeared into the impenetrable shadows along the sides of the great room.

I had paused to take my shot, but I now moved forwards, cursing Lestrade's clumsiness as I did so. Next moment my own foot fell on something which broke beneath it, emitting the same sharp cracking sound, and I heard the same noise from the direction of both Holmes and the Major.

'Nutshells!' exclaimed Holmes. 'A simple but effective alarm surrounding his living space. Well, gentlemen, this is not going to be as easy as we had expected.'

From somewhere in the darkness in front of us I heard that sinister guttural chuckle that had chilled my blood in the pit in Hampshire.

Chapter Twenty-six

Battle in the Dark

It may have been the view of Sherlock Holmes that our proposed capture of the Apache would be easy, but it had never been mine, and Holmes's comment only served to underline the difficulties that now faced us.

Before we had triggered his simple alarms we had known where he was and he had been unaware of our presence. It might not have been unreasonable to suppose that the four of us, armed and able, could rush him and overpower him, though I fully expected that one or more of us might suffer serious injury from such a clever and determined opponent.

Now the advantage lay entirely with him. We had only the vaguest idea of his whereabouts, while he knew, fairly certainly, that we lay in the four passages between the rows of goods. The sound of our feet on his nutshells and the shots fired would have confirmed that there were four of us, though he might not realise that we were all armed.

Across the ends of the walkways in which we hid was a wider passage, from side to side of the floor. Beyond that it was about one hundred feet to the windows, an area stacked, seemingly at random, with boxes, chests and barrels. Their presence filled the ground ahead of us with shadows, in any one of which our quarry might be lurking. For all we knew, he might be lying just across the wide transverse path, hidden deep in shadow, while he prepared a knife, an arrow or even a bullet for one of us.

'What next, Mr Holmes?' Major Braithwaite asked. 'Shall I go across and chase him out?'

'Certainly not, Major,' said Holmes. 'You know the dangers of that. The moon will have risen and the fireworks will soon end. When they do, the shadows beyond us will cease to shift and it will be more possible to define where abouts he is hiding. Once we can do that, we can consider what means are necessary to extract him.'

This exchange must have been heard by the Apache, though how much of it he understood I cannot say. I lay for what seemed to be several minutes in the darkness, well concealed behind the bales that lined both sides of my gangway. Suddenly I felt a touch on my leg and Holmes's voice whispered 'Watson!' very softly from behind me.

I turned round, to find him crouching in the gangway at my back, his finger to his lips. 'At any moment the fireworks will cease,' he said. 'You heard my reply to Major Braithwaite. When I start firing, I expect each of you to follow me, in turn, but after the first round you will have to do my firing for me.'

'Where are you going?' I hissed, though I thought I knew the answer.

'I am going to work my way across into his area and try to establish where he is hiding,' he replied.

'That will be hideously dangerous,' I protested. 'Why do we not send Lestrade down to summon reinforcements by way of the hoists?'

'Because it would take no end of time to raise any

worthwhile force by the hoists and long before we had done so he would realise what we were up to. No – we must smoke him out ourselves.'

'What, exactly, do you want me to do?' I asked.

'I shall fire the first round. When I have done so, you follow suit, then Braithwaite, then Lestrade. Then you fire again, making sure that he cannot see the flare of your pistol – fire from cover. Then wait a couple of seconds and fire again, then Braithwaite, then Lestrade, and so on.'

'It won't work, Holmes,' I objected. 'He will realise that there are only three of us firing.'

'He will not do so for a short time and that is all I need,' he whispered and slid away into the darkness.

I waited again and, as my friend had predicted, the rattle of fireworks and the glow from the river died away, leaving us only the moon's faint light through the distant, grimy windows.

A shot sounded from my left and I followed suit, placing a shot into one of the pools of shadow that lay between us and the windows. All of us responded as Holmes had planned and, before the third round of shots was complete, I detected signs of movement on the far left. I ceased fire, for fear of hitting Holmes, and Major Braithwaite called out something in a strange tongue.

He was answered by that disturbing laugh that I had heard before. 'Speak your own tongue, white man!' a voice cried. 'You have no right to speak mine.'

'I know your voice,' called Braithwaite. 'Are you not Eskishay?'

There was a silent pause, then the laugh again. 'Long Face,' the voice said, 'I know your voice too. What does a bluecoat major do in the land of the Great Queen? Why do you help the Queen's men to hunt me?'

'You have broken the Great Queen's law,' answered

the Major. 'You have killed her people. You must stand trial for these things.'

'It is good that the Great Queen would give me a trial, Long Face. That is more than the Americans would give me. But I want no trial. I have done what I had to for my people.'

'Your people are at peace with the white men,' said Braithwaite. 'You have broken the law.'

'My people are dying at San Carlos,' the Apache replied, 'and Crook, who always spoke truth to us, is dead. You spoke truth to us, Long Face, but you went with Crook. Now our children die and the agents steal from us, and nobody hears our complaints.'

'How will you help your people by murdering the Great Queen's people?'

'They say that the Great Queen's people have always been good to my people, but the Americans have not. They have taken all our land that is not desert or mountains, so they can grow their grass and trees and fruit, so they can dig mines and build houses, so they can make railroads and telegraphs. They have left us nothing but the desert and the mountains, and the land at San Carlos. They drive us to Florida and to Alabama, where the land stinks with fever. We will not go. If all we have is the mountains and the desert we will keep them and live there. But the Americans are not happy with what they have stolen. They want the gold of the mountains, and if they have it, they will come in thousands once more, so that even the mountains will not hide us. I have killed those who knew where the gold is. When I have the map of the gold I shall be finished. I shall go back to my mountains.'

'You cannot go back to your mountains,' said the Major. 'You have killed against the law. You have murdered one of the Queen's bluecoats. You must stand your trial.'

'There will be no trial, Long Face. You will kill me or I shall kill you and your friends.'

'I do not wish to kill you, Eskishay Once we were friends. Once you were a loyal scout for General Crook. Why should I wish to kill you?'

'Crook is dead and his words are as dust. I followed Crook because he told us truth, but when he was gone they took his scouts and sent us to prison. They put us in trains like cattle and sent us to jail. I escaped and made my way to the mountains. There some of us survived and there they will stay. Indian Tommy was once our friend – more, he was one of our tribe – but he lied and he stole, and he fought his friends. So we turned him back to his own people when we might have killed him, and he repaid our kindness by betraying us for gold.'

'I am not like Indian Tommy, Eskishay. Crook was not like Indian Tommy. Why do you war against us still?'

'I have said, Long Face, we have nothing left except our mountains and the gold that is in those mountains. We shall never let the Americans have our gold. Because Indian Tommy betrayed us I was sent to find him and bring home his map. When I have killed, it was those who helped to steal our gold or those who stood in my way. You are a warrior, Long Face. You too have killed the enemies of your people. You swore your oath to your Great White Chief in Washington. I have sworn mine to my chief, and he has sent me to avenge my people and to take back the map. If I cannot do that, then I must die, and if I will not surrender, then you must kill me.'

'That is your wish,' said Braithwaite. 'It is not why we are here. If you will surrender, Eskishay, the Great Queen will see that you have a fair trial.'

'You have always spoken truth, Long Face, as Crook always spoke truth, but they made a liar of Crook, so that his heart was broken and he left the Army. They will make a liar of you, too, Long Face.'

Lestrade's voice intervened, calling loudly, 'I am an Inspector of the Metropolitan Police of Her Majesty Queen Victoria. I tell you now, in the hearing of Major Braithwaite, whose word you respect, that you may surrender to us and your life will be protected and you will be given a fair trial.'

'So that I may be hanged,' said the Indian. 'I believe you, Englishman. You are a servant of the Great Queen, but I would rather die by a bullet than on the end of a white man's rope.'

Through all this exchange I had been peering into the gloom, striving to locate the voice that answered Braithwaite and understanding that the Major was trying to prolong the conversation in order to give Holmes a better chance of locating the Apache. I was fairly certain that I had worked out which pool of darkness hid Eskishay from our eyes, when I became aware of a new pool of shadow on top of a stack of crates. It moved slightly and I realised that Holmes was crouching above the Indian, awaiting his moment to pounce.

Major Braithwaite was calling, 'Eskishay. You have heard the police officer. You can trust his word. You can surrender yourself with honour. There are not just us few here. There are a hundred of the Queen's bluecoats below. You cannot escape from here.'

Eskishay chuckled again. 'Long Face, old friend. You and I have talked and we have fought, since you were a boy at Camp Grant. I trust your word as I would trust Crook's, but there will be no rope for me. The moment has come to finish talking and it is time for our final fight, Long Face.'

He had barely spoken the last word when Holmes plunged down on to him from his eyrie atop the crates. Braithwaite, Lestrade and I sprang to our feet and raced across the warehouse's gangway into the area where the battle was, unable to see what was happening but hearing blows and strangled cries from the darkness.

A moment later our problem was reversed, as the dim, grimy windows of the warehouse suddenly flared with brilliant light. For a few seconds I was both blinded and confused, then I realised that Holmes's firework display having ended, the River Police launches had adjusted their powerful electric lamps to illuminate the upper part of the warehouse.

Now we could see that Holmes and the Apache were wrestling on the floor, rolling and struggling amid the barrels and bales that littered the area. None of us dared to take a shot, for fear of hitting Holmes, but all three of us moved towards the scene of the struggle. I looked around for Holmes's dark lantern and, seeing it standing where Holmes had hidden in the gangway, motioned to Lestrade to bring it with us.

Holmes and the Indian were evenly matched. My friend was taller and armed with his skills in baritsu, but the stocky Indian was muscular in the arms and legs, and broad in the chest, giving as good as he got. Nevertheless, even his stamina was unequal to the resources of Sherlock Holmes. At last the Apache began to show signs of exhaustion and to respond less vigorously to Holmes's manoeuvres, so that there came a time when Holmes knelt on top of him, holding him down while the Indian made no response.

'Lestrade,' Holmes commanded, 'bring the lantern and your handcuffs.'

Lestrade stepped forward and drew his manacles from his pocket. As he did so the Apache writhed like an eel under Holmes's grip, slid from beneath him and sprang up, smashing the lantern from Lestrade's hand and bursting between Braithwaite and me.

I know not whether his escape was a planned device, or whether he took advantage of a momentary lapse in our concentration. As the lantern shattered, I spun and took a quick shot at the fleeing man, without success. I leapt after him, followed by the other three, but he was already plunging into the stairwell. I followed him to the stair's entrance and would have climbed after him, but a knife whirred past my ear and discouraged me, so that I stopped until Holmes and the others had joined me.

Apart from Holmes, we were cursing our carelessness in allowing the escape, but Holmes merely drew the knife from its resting place in the floorboards. 'It was thrown from above,' he remarked. 'He is taking to the roof.'

Chapter Twenty-seven

The Song of Death

We were none of us without courage. All of us had taken our chances in battle before, with various opponents, but I do not believe that any one of the four of us – even Holmes himself – was anxious to be the first to venture into that dark stairway.

Nevertheless, Holmes did and we followed. It was still pitch-dark, for the light from the police launches could not penetrate the stairwell, but we could step ahead with some confidence, so long as we had assured ourselves that Eskishay was not waiting to ambush us at some dark turn of the steps.

Holmes leaned into the stairway and fired two rounds upwards. The echo of the shots died away and he said, 'He is not there. If he is not on the upper floor, he will have made for the roof.'

'At least he will be unarmed,' remarked Lestrade.

'Do not depend upon it,' said Holmes. 'Remember the nutshells. This man has provided against attack from any direction. He will not have ignored the roof and he may have weapons hidden above us.'

With that gloomy intelligence we set out up the dark

stairs. We were soon on the warehouse's upper floor. Like the floor below, it was scattered with bales, barrels and crates, though not in such profusion. We stood at the stairhead and scanned the dark area around us.

'Is he here, do you think?' I asked Holmes.

He shook his head. 'If I understand him aright,' he said, 'he was telling Braithwaite that this was his last stand – that he would conquer or die here. I do not believe that he seeks another inconclusive contest like the one below. He will have made for the roof. There is the end – there it is as far as he can go and there he must subdue us or die in the attempt. Am I right, Major?'

The American nodded. 'That seems like the way he would think,' he agreed. 'He will certainly not surrender to us and he told us the reasons why – he will not end on a white man's rope. He will face us, kill as many as he can, then accept his own death. That will be the way that he sees the position. At the same time, he may see that his only chance of escape lies in the Thames. He cannot leave this building by the ground floor – Inspector Lestrade's battalions have it surrounded – but a plunge to the river, in the dark, would give him at least an even chance of getting away. Be very careful when you emerge on to the roof, gentlemen, because he will be waiting for us and he will be armed.'

It was evidently impossible for us to return to the roof through the skylight by which we had entered the building. It was too far above us and we would have been exposed to any attack, inasmuch as each of us would have had to climb out separately. Instead, Holmes showed us a broad flight of wooden steps that led to two wide timber doors set in the roof. Each door was kept closed by two sturdy bolts, though these had obviously not been used for a while.

'They will make a devil of a noise,' objected Lestrade.

'So they will,' agreed Holmes, 'but if we can draw two

bolts simultaneously we can be on the rooftop in a flash. In addition, these doors are surrounded above by a low brick wall, which will afford us a little cover.'

'Still,' said Lestrade, 'he cannot avoid hearing the bolts drawn. He will be ready for us before we're out there.'

'Then we had best be smart about our exit, Lestrade,' said Holmes imperturbably. 'Do you fancy the alternative?' And he pointed to where a drift of smoke was coiling out of the stairs to the lower floor. 'This building is very likely to share its neighbour's fate in the near future and the only practical way out is from the roof. Shall we move, gentlemen?'

With all four of us heaving together the bolts were easily drawn, though they made the noise that Lestrade had predicted. As soon as the door was free we heaved it wide open and, pistols drawn, sprang out.

No sooner were we in the open than an arrow hummed past our heads, rapidly followed by two more. Even as I flung myself flat on the bolted door, I reflected at the extraordinary speed with which the Apache could nock an arrow into his bow and fire.

All four of us lay on the wooden door. As Holmes had said, the two doors were surrounded by a low wall, only a few bricks high, which provided a very small degree of cover.

Cautiously Holmes raised his head above that small battlement and fired a shot. 'He is in that direction.' He pointed towards the river. 'But he is difficult to see.'

Each of us in turn risked a quick view over the wall. Every one of our movements drew another arrow, skimming low across the little wall. I began to fear that he had us helplessly pinned down. The moon was obscured by clouds so that we had lost its feeble light.

It was Major Braithwaite who spied our enemy. 'There is a wooden structure in that corner,' he said, pointing. 'A ventilator housing, I think. He is behind that, in the space between it and the parapet of the roof. Only the searchlights are preventing him from leaping into the river. Eskishay,' he shouted, 'you cannot escape. You see the lights on the river? The Queen's bluecoats are below, with boats and guns. If you jump they will take you. It is best that you surrender to me now.'

'Never,' came the reply. 'I have said, Long Face, that I will kill you all or die here.'

'He will not have many arrows,' commented Holmes. 'Once he has run out, we might rush him from both sides. In the meantime we should encourage him to use up his ammunition by showing ourselves as possible targets.'

For what seemed to be a long time we continued taking single shots in the direction of the wooden hut that concealed Eskishay and again each movement of ours sent an arrow whirring towards us. More than once he came within inches of wounding one of us.

Clouds of smoke had begun to rise from the open hatch beside us and we wondered how long we could maintain our position, now that the warehouse seemed to be well alight below us. It must have been the fire that summoned reinforcements, for soon we heard the rattling of both chain hoists moving into action.

'Your men appear to be taking a hand,' Holmes remarked to Lestrade, 'but they will be in difficulty. From his position he can pick them off at either of the hoist platforms.'

Our exchange of bullets and arrows continued, while the steady creak of the hoists told us that the platforms had gone down and were on the way back.

'The best possible moment to effect a rush', remarked Holmes, 'will be when the hoists arrive. He cannot fire in three directions at once. As soon as the hoists reach the roof, Watson and I will take him from the right and Lestrade and the Major from the left. That increases his targets to four.'

We heard the hoists stop and crouched behind our little battlement, waiting to plunge across the darkened rooftop.

'Now!' shouted Holmes and we sprang up, racing towards the wooden hut, firing as we went. I caught a glimpse of dark figures tumbling over the parapet of the roof and heard the hum of arrows.

A police officer must have turned a lantern's beam on the ventilator, for I saw Eskishay, crouched at the side of it, flinging away his bow and drawing a knife from his belt. It was only a second's glimpse, for the ventilator suddenly disgorged a dense cloud of black smoke that rolled down around it, concealing the Apache from view and driving us back, choking and coughing, as it spread across the roof.

'Where is he? Where is he?' called Lestrade. 'He'll get away yet!'

That was unlikely. More and more constables appeared, the hoist platforms having been crowded to their absolute capacity, but still there was no sign of Eskishay.

Suddenly a pillar of flame shot from the ventilator, sucking the smoke upwards in its draught. By its light we saw the Indian, tongues of fire about him where his clothing had caught light, staggering towards the roof's parapet. From his mouth came a long, ululating chant.

'The death chant,' said Braithwaite. 'He knows it's over.'

We watched as he clambered on to the parapet and stood for a moment, the flames from his garments streaming upwards; then, without a break in his chant, he plunged downwards.

Rushing to the edge, we were in time to see the flaming figure hurtle into the Thames and disappear. Quickly the police on the launches turned their powerful lights on the surface, but nothing could be seen of Eskishay.

'If we are to get off this roof safely,' said Lestrade, 'we must move now.'

All four of us crowded the first platform to go down and it was not very long before we stood in Brewers Lane. One of Lestrade's men brought us a four-wheeler. Lestrade was remaining at the scene. The warehouse was now well alight, fire engines had arrived and a considerable crowd was assembled.

We took our farewell of Major Braithwaite at his hotel, expressing our thanks for his participation.

He grinned at us. 'When I see old Danziger in Phoenix and he asks how it went in London,' he said, 'he's not going to believe that I fought my last Apache on a rooftop in the middle of your city, but I wouldn't have missed it, gentlemen. It's a dandy of a tale for my grandchildren.'

Back at Baker Street, we took a quick supper and retired. I cannot speak for Holmes who, despite his avoidance of exercise, had the most remarkable muscular and nervous resources, but I was profoundly exhausted.

Next morning I found my friend up before me. He was seated at the table, poring over the curious leather map but, when Mrs Hudson began to serve our breakfast, he rolled it up and dropped it back on to his writing desk.

'You have not solved it, then?' I remarked.

He shook his head. 'Perhaps it should not be solved,' he said. 'Enough men have been lured to their deaths by the Peralta mine. Nevertheless, I am sure that a solution is possible. What the mind of one man can devise, the mind of another may unravel and I cannot escape the feeling that there is something about that map that I have overlooked.'

We had completed breakfast, and Mrs Hudson was clearing away, when she paused and picked up something from the carpet. She looked at it closely, then held it out to me. 'What on earth is that, Doctor?' she asked and I saw that she held one of the little leather flowers that decorated the Peralta map.

'It is a decoration from something that Holmes has been working on,' I told her and took it from her, turning it over in my hands. For several seconds I did not register what I had seen; then, 'Holmes!', I cried, 'Look!' and I showed him the back of the little piece of leather.

'Upon my word!' he exclaimed, whipping his lens from his coat pocket and examining the leather. 'You have it, Watson! You have it!' He leapt from his chair, seized the map and unrolled it across the table. Quickly he turned over each of the leather decorations in turn. On the back of each one was impressed a tiny symbol – one of the symbols on Crosby's list. In some cases there were two symbols.

Holmes stood back from the map, a broad smile on his face. 'As simple as that!' he remarked. He pointed with a long finger. 'Here are the Superstitions, here is the Silver King Mine, here is Weaver's Needle, there is Apache Junction, there the Green Spring, there is Superior, there a door in the mountain wall and there a box canyon. Most particularly,' he went on, placing his finger firmly on a spot in the Superstition Mountains, 'there is the Peralta mine!'

'What will you do with it?' I asked, thinking of the long tale of misery that the search for the mine had engendered.

'I shall have it framed,' he said, 'with Crosby's key pasted to its back. Then I shall send it to Mrs Crosby.'

'You will not reveal to her what it means?' I asked.

'Of course not,' he replied. 'This singular piece of

craftsmanship deserves to be admired, but its meaning may remain a secret for me.'

That is precisely what he did. Whether that curious picture hangs still on the walls of Bradon Lodge, whether it has been consigned to an attic or a bonfire with the passage of time, or whether it has gone to some village charitable sale, I know not but, like Holmes, I am quite satisfied that the secret of the Peralta mine should remain lost.

Editor's Notes

As explained in my introductory Note, I have made such efforts as seemed reasonable to try to establish the authenticity of this manuscript. As to the document itself, a text in blue-black ink, handwritten on sheets of cream foolscap, I refer you to my observations on Watson's manuscripts in my notes on *Sherlock Holmes and the Harvest of Death* (Constable, 1999). There is, however, one point which I should explain. In my introduction and in previous volumes I have asserted that there is no unassailable specimen of Watson's handwriting extant. Readers have taken issue with me, pointing out that what seems to be Watson's writing appears on a plan published in the *Strand* magazine in February 1904 as an illustration to the 'The Priory School'. However, what is evidently the same writing appears on a plan published with 'The Naval Treaty', where the plan was supposedly drawn by Watson's schoolfriend Percy Phelps, and on a plan in 'The Golden Pince-nez', apparently drawn by Stanley Hopkins. Dorothy Sayers deals with the issues of the three plans in 'The Dates in the Red-Headed League', a paper which originally appeared in her anthology *Unpopular Opinions* and was reprinted in *Seventeen Steps to Baker Street*, edited by James Holroyd (George Allen & Unwin, 1967). She suggests that Watson supplied three scruffy plans to the printer, who had them redrawn for block-making purposes. In support of her argument (which I adopt entirely) she points out that the signature 'John H. Watson' was eliminated from the 'Priory School' plan in the omnibus edition of the works in 1928.

My notes here merely record the results of my efforts to check the truth of Watson's statements and try to establish that the text is a document written by him in the early 1920s and not a modern forgery (it is shaming to record that there is a virtual industry in the production of forged Watson manuscripts at the present). I do not pretend that my researches have been anywhere near complete and those with more time or greater expertise may be more successful.

Chapter One

It is often assumed that Holmes's references to the Head Lama are meant to indicate the Dalai Lama, but this was not so. Lord Donegall, in a paper for the *New Strand*, reprinted in the James Holroyd anthology referred to above, points out that, at the time of Holmes's incursion into Tibet, the Dalai Lama was an infant and the Regency was exercised by the Abbot of Ten-Gyeling, known as the Head Lama. Donegall further speculates on the difficulty of foreigners gaining access to Tibet at that time and suggests that Mycroft Holmes had arranged matters so that Sherlock might carry out a diplomatic mission in Tibet, which was under great pressure from the British Empire's enemy of those days – Russia.

Holmes is, as usual, right about the complex knots of the Quipu. There is an entire branch of mathematics dealing with knots, one that has traditionally been regarded as purely academic until recently. Now the work of mathematicians is being used to assist biologists' attempts to unravel the knots created by viral enzymes when they enter the body of the host.

Perfumed Anti-Zymotic Crystals were produced by the London Patent Automatic Disinfection Company to sweeten the toilets of sporting yachts.

Chapter Two

Aldhous and Rushbrook of Brightlingsea were builders of both yachts and fishing boats, remaining in business until 1962. At least one of their Victorian yachts is still afloat, though much rebuilt. Perhaps the best remembered of their vessels is none of their sporting winners but the *Mignonette*, which sank in the South Atlantic in 1884. Its crew escaped in a boat but, after weeks without food, the cabin boy, Richard Parker, was killed and eaten. Shortly afterwards the survivors were rescued. Captain Dudley and Edwin Stephens were tried for the boy's murder and sentenced to death, though the sentences were converted to a short term of imprisonment. The case remains the basis in English law for the proposition that you may not kill an innocent party solely to save your own life. See *Cannibalism and the Common Law* by A. W. Brian Simpson (University of Chicago, 1984, King Penguin, 1986).

Chapter Four

I cannot, alas, establish where and when Holmes met Bat Masterson, but many commentators believe that Holmes spent some time in the USA as a young man and in another of the Watson manuscripts that I have edited it becomes apparent that the detective also knew Buffalo Bill Cody well (see *Sherlock Holmes and the Royal Flush*, Constable, 1998).

The Western gunslingers' practice of 'fanning' a pistol is described (with diagram) in volume two of Eugene

Cunningham's *TriggerNometry: A Gallery of Master Gun-fighters with Technical Notes too on Leather Slapping as a Fine Art* (Press of the Pioneers Inc., 1934, Caxton Prin-ters, 1941, NEL Foursquare, 1967, 1978).

The gunslinger referred to by Holmes was most prob-ably Charley Harrison, a skilful gambler who escaped Salt Lake City seconds ahead of a Mormon lynch party and established himself successfully on the Colorado goldfield. Eugene Teats who, as a ten-year-old, was taught to shoot by Harrison, recorded that Harrison could put two and sometimes three bullet holes into a thrown can, so fast and accurate was his action – 'and that with either hand or with both guns at once'. Bat Masterson commented that Harrison was, 'with all his dazzling speed . . . the most brilliant pistol handler I ever saw, and a far more deadly shot than most of the great gunfighters'. George F. Willison, in *Here They Dug the Gold* (Eyre & Spottiswoode, 1952), confirms that Har-rison used cap-and-ball weapons and calls him, 'the most accomplished gunman in the West'. During the Civil War Harrison joined the Confederate States Army and was killed by Indians while with the Army. Eugene Cunningham (see above) records that John Wesley Hardin, who was credited with more than forty kills with a pistol, also preferred cap-and-ball weapons for speed and accuracy.

Crossing the Line certificates have been awarded since nobody knows when to seagoers (passengers or crew) crossing the Equator for the first time. In the full cere-mony, a man dressed as Neptune accompanied by a 'Court' of ludicrously dressed mermaids and mermen appears on deck as the vessel reaches the Equator, exam-ines candidates and subjects them to various pranks, usually including having a shave by King Neptune's barber, after which certificates are awarded. I have pho-tographs of the custom being honoured aboard a Royal Naval vessel in the Pacific in 1929 and have seen film of the ceremony being performed aboard troopships bound for the Falklands War in 1982. I blush to confess that my own Crossing certificate was awarded by Qantas Airlines aboard one of their jets in 1961. We were not boarded by Neptune.

Ye Olde Whorehouse did actually exist in San Francisco's Sacramento Street but I have been unable to confirm whether a Madame Lu-Ann practised in Demerara. Holmes Street was part of the area known as Tiger Bay in Demerara, though it had no apparent connection with the Great Detective. Nobody seems to know which of the world's three Tiger Bays (in Demerara, Cardiff and London) was the original.

Chapters Five and Six
The treasure-hunting expedition referred to by both Mrs Crosby and Captain Napley certainly took place. In August 1888 a yacht called *Alerte* left Southampton with a small professional crew and a party of 'gentleman adventurers', nine of whom had paid the organiser one hundred pounds each for a tenth share of the venture. The organiser was Edward Frederick Knight (1852–1925) barrister, novelist, canoeist, yachtsman, treasure hunter and war correspondent. Knight had heard of a treasure-hunting expedition that had set out from Tyneside for Trinidad Island – not the better-known West Indian island but Trinidad Island which lies a thousand miles south-east of its namesake and seven hundred miles east of Brazil in the South Atlantic.

The Tyneside party failed to find gold, but Knight extracted from the organiser what was known of the hoard. It was said to be the plate and jewels of the cathedral at Lima, shipped out during a revolution in 1821 and captured by pirates who had hidden it on Trinidad Island. Knight's party called in at the Salvage Islands (between Madeira and the Canaries), having heard of a hoard concealed there, but found nothing. In

February of 1890 he returned to Britain, having spent months in exploration and excavation at Trinidad without success. In the same year he published *The Cruise of the Alerte* (reprinted Granada Publishing, 1984), a fascinating account of his expedition, in which, although he does not identify his 'gentleman adventurers', he does remark that two of his original selection dropped out just before the voyage.

For those of you interested in treasure-hunting, Knight's book contains all that he knew or deduced about the treasure's whereabouts, together with maps of the Salvage Islands and Trinidad Island. I should warn you, though, that F. George Kay, who saw Trinidad Island briefly in the 1920s, wrote about it thirty years later as, 'a mass of loathsome, disintegrating volcanic rock which, to me, gives an ominous impression of the world in its death throes'. He quoted a survey in the early twentieth century, which called the island 'rotten to the heart', and went on to describe how, 'Masses of volcanic rock have slithered into the sea, as if the island had been used as a huge tip-truck'. He described the fierce land crabs of the island, which will attack men (confirmed by Knight), and said that all water on Trinidad was poisonous (not confirmed by Knight) but also remarked that 'Almost without doubt an immense treasure lies buried on this crab-infested island'. For his complete text, see 'Treasure Islands of the Atlantic' (*Wide World* magazine, November 1957). You should also be warned that the treasure of Lima is sometimes alleged to be one of the treasures concealed on Cocos Island.

Chapter Eight
The Apache arrow, with a shaft of dried reed, triple-feathered and pointed with a triangular quartz head, is described in *Bury My Heart at Wounded Knee* by Dee Brown (Barrie & Jenkins, 1972, Pan, 1974, Picador, 1975) as light in weight but of great penetrative power.

Chapter Ten

Of all Watson's concealments, none seems to have caused more argument than his use of the address '221b Baker Street', because there is not and has never been a 221 on London's Baker Street. All manner of explanations have been attempted, some suggesting that the real address was never on Baker Street and others adopt various buildings on Baker Street as their preferred locale. Michael Harrison, in *The London of Sherlock Holmes* (David & Charles, 1972) avoids the dispute, but points out that, wherever it was, 221b must have been above a ground-floor shop – 221a – a not entirely convincing argument inasmuch as 221a might have been an office. He prints a photograph of 109 Baker Street, deemed by some to be the real 221, and points out that it is the last surviving original frontage on the street. His photograph bears out Holmes's description of the building's front, but does not show a ground-floor shop as described in the present narrative. It can be seen, then, that either 109 was not the original 221 or the present text is spurious.

In *The Backyards of Baker Street*, a magnificently argued paper based on superb research, which appeared first in the *Sherlock Holmes Journal* and was reprinted in the James Holroyd anthology cited above, Bernard Davies establishes Number 31 (on the west side of Baker Street, in the block between George Street and King Street) as the most likely original for 221.

Chapter Eleven

Nick Musgrove of the University of Wolverhampton has been kind enough to check Wan Fat's information about rattlesnakes for me and confirms that the Chinese shopkeeper was correct. America boasts some seventy subspecies of the snake, most of them (despite Western movies) not seriously poisonous, only about one in five hundred bites proving fatal. Nevertheless, it has been noted in recent years that the milder varieties are becoming more venomous. In Alabama in 1998 a preacher from that bizarre Baptist sect that handles rattlesnakes as a part of its worship died within ten minutes of being bitten. A soldier, bitten in Florida, only survived after the application of forty vials of anti-venom, as against the usual five to ten, while a student, bitten in California, required thirty-five vials to save him. Experts differ as to the cause of the increased power. Some believe that hybrids are occurring between more and lesser poisonous varieties, increasing the danger of the lesser breeds; others assert that ground squirrels and other rodents normally killed by rattlers are developing enzymes, which break down rattler poison in their blood, forcing the snakes to become more venomous in order to survive. A third group points to the effect of humans on the snakes. Round-ups of mature rattlesnakes, like the big festival held at Sweetwater, Texas, annually, increase the percentage of younger snakes (which are more poisonous) in the wild. Incidentally, the meat of the snakes killed at Sweetwater is barbecued and eaten. Neither Nick Musgrove nor I have tested Wan Fat's recipe for fried diamond-back with ginger, water chestnuts and spring onions.

The Moqui Indian ceremony with rattlesnakes put into the celebrant's mouth is described in Captain J. Bourke's *On the Border With Crook* (Charles Scribner, 1891, Time-Life, 1974).

Chapter Twelve

Portmadoc in north Wales was turned from an insignificant fishing hamlet into a commercial port by a nineteenth-century entrepreneur called Maddocks, after whom it is named. He built the town's long 'cob', reclaiming land, establishing a decent harbour and allowing the town to become a centre of small boat building and commercial coastal shipping, much of it from the slate quarries of the area. Nowadays it has become, coincidentally, a yachting centre.

Welsh legend asserts that, in about 1170, a Prince Madoc sailed from Wales in a ship called *Gwennan Gorn* and discovered a great island beyond the 'sea of weed' – presumably Bermuda, beyond the Sargasso Sea. It is also said that he set out on a second voyage with three ships and never returned. Colonial America was full of stories of a pale-skinned Indian tribe who used Welsh words and preserved ancient Welsh manuscripts, and these were often said to be the descendants of Madoc's party. For example, Francis Lewis, a signatory to the Declaration of Independence, recorded that, captured by Indians and about to be burned alive, he was spared when his captors found he spoke Welsh, a language which they understood. In 1792, when Britain, Spain and France were competing for territory in North America, attempts were made to establish this Welsh claim to discovery of the south-eastern territories then held by Spain and France. One John Evans, a Welshman, was sent to America to examine the evidence and subsequently reported that there was no truth in the 'Welsh Indian' legend. For this reason, and because there was no Prince Madoc known to history, modern commentators have tended to reject the story. However, in 1960 a Sussex saleroom sold an ancient manuscript, which turned out to be a twelfth-century list of missing vessels. It reveals that there was a Madoc who sailed in 1171 in a ship recorded as *Guignon Gorn* and failed to return. Richard Deacon, in *Madoc and the Discovery of America* (Frederick Muller, 1967) cites references to Madoc in ancient Welsh documents, suggests that he may have been an illegitimate son of Owain Gwynnedd and points out that Evans, after reporting that there was no truth in the story, stayed across the Atlantic (where he could not be arrested for treason), accepting an office of profit under the Spanish colonial administration before drinking himself to death. Perhaps the Welsh did discover North America, along with the Viking Leif Erikson, the monk Nicholas of Lynne, Saint Brendan, the Orcadian Prince Henry Sinclair, the Basques, the Bretons and almost everyone else in Europe except Columbus! Certainly the modern Mandan Indians assert that they have Welsh ancestry.

The signatory to the telegram from Tombstone seems to have been the well-known gunfighter, cattleman and lawman Texas John Slaughter, who became sheriff of Cochise County with his headquarters at Tombstone in the years after the commercial and political corruption of Sheriff Behan and Marshall Earp.

Chapter Fourteen

'Shavetail', an expression still used in the US Services, refers to a newly created, inexperienced lieutenant, but its origin goes back to the cavalry's operations against the Indians of the south-west in which Major Braithwaite was involved. Supplies for cavalry columns were carried on mules and when a new, untrained mule was added to the column, the mule drivers would shave its tail, either completely or so as to leave only a tuft on the end, the 'shavetail' serving as a warning to men behind the mule on a narrow mountain trail that its behaviour was untried and unpredictable.

I have been unable to identify Major Braithwaite as serving in Arizona Territory with the Third Cavalry. John G. Bourke, who himself served under General Crook in Arizona, on the Rosebud and again in Arizona, wrote a memoir of his service, *On the Border with Crook* (Charles Scribner, 1891, Time-Life, 1974) in which he lists all the officers of the Third and Fifth Cavalry and Twenty-third Infantry who were concerned in Crook's two Arizona campaigns, but there is no Braithwaite. It is evidently one of Watson's pseudonyms.

Braithwaite is right in remarking that everyone remembers Custer and nobody recalls George Crook. Crook was the most successful of all the senior officers sent West during the long years of war against the redskins on the Western frontier. A skilful soldier, who was always ready to fight when he had to, Crook never-theless understood and sympathised with the redskins and sought to improve their lot. As Commandant of the Army in Arizona, he took over administration of reser-vations from the Department of the Interior, because he was well aware that a frequent cause of unrest among the Apaches was dishonesty and bullying by the gov-ernment agents on the reservations. This move made him deeply unpopular with the clique in Washington who grew rich by having dishonest friends and relatives appointed as agents in order to defraud the Indians. Nevertheless, he succeeded in persuading the Arizona Grand Jury to pass an indictment against a corrupt agent and send him for trial. When Crook was reassigned to Arizona, to end Geronimo's uprising, he was the victim of endless sniping in Washington. When he finally achieved a deal with the Apaches, which would have ended the uprising, he was reprimanded and the government backed down on his deal. Crook resigned and died only a few years later.

Unlike the flamboyant Custer, with his tailored uni-forms, high boots and shoulder-length hair, Crook rarely wore uniform, preferring a linen suit and a pith helmet for desert wear, as he preferred a mule to a horse as a mount. He was a soft-spoken, unswearing man who, in his spare time, studied the birds and wildlife of the areas where he campaigned.

Chapter Fifteen

Braithwaite's story of the attempted arrest of Cochise is true. John G. Bourke, in the work cited above, charges

218

Bascom's account heavily, saying that the Lieutenant's ill-considered action was responsible for 'Ten thousand men, women, and children killed, wounded, or tortured to death, scared out of their senses or driven out of the country, their wagon and pack-trains run off and destroyed, ranchos ruined, and all industrial development stopped'.

The Irish–Mexican boy kidnapped, Micky Free, grew up – despite the loss of an eye in a hunting accident – to be an army scout. His photograph appears in *Fighting Indians of the West* by Martin F. Schmitt and Dee Brown (Charles Scribner, 1948) along with a comment on him by the famous chief of the army scouts, Al Sieber, who apparently described Free as 'half-Mexican, half-Irish and whole son of a bitch', which may account for Braithwaite's remark about him.

Chapter Sixteen

Edmund Danziger is, apparently, one of Watson's invented names, but it is possible to identify him with a Simon Nordinger, who shared the features of his career and was a successful businessman in Phoenix in the 1890s. Nordinger owned a hay ranch at Tulare, California, where he employed a teenage boy who had lived among the Indians and who told him about the Peralta mine. Whether the boy who worked for Nordinger was called Indian Tommy and became a Tombstone gunslinger is not known.

The saga of the Peralta mine is mentioned in various books on lost treasures and mines, but perhaps the most interesting is by Ely Sims. Sims lived in Arizona from the 1890s and for six decades sought the mine and accumulated information about it. In 1953 he wrote his book, *The Lost Dutchman Mine*, using the name by which it was then called. The book was published in Britain by Eyre & Spottiswoode in about 1956.

Chapter Seventeen

While it might be assumed that much of Major Braithwaite's information is simply 'old soldiers' tales', a great deal of what he said can be checked against information in Ely Sims's book cited above. Sims tells the same story of Don Miguel Peralta and the two Dutchmen, and the story of Dr Thorne, though he also tells how Thorne returned to Arizona in the 1880s and tried to find the mine. He failed, although he found the ruins and the view of Weaver's Needle where the Indians permitted him to pick up ore. Sims points out that the area is subject to earthquakes and suggests that, between Thorne's two visits, seismological events had changed the landscape and concealed the mine, accounting for the failure to rediscover it since the 1880s.

The principal difference between Sims's account and that given by Major Braithwaite is in the story of the two ex-soldiers. Sims tells how the body of the first one was found, but does not mention a missing head, nor does he mention the finding of a second body, with or without a head. He suggests that the youths were ambushed and killed, not by Indians, but by a Pinal man who had heard them talking about their find and knew that they set out for the mine carrying several hundred dollars.

Sims does, however, recount occasions when searchers for the mine lost their heads. Dr Erwin C. Ruth worked as a government vet, examining Mexican cattle imported into Texas. In this capacity he heard of the Peralta mine and was, allegedly, given an old map of the site by a Peralta descendant. He passed his information to his father, Adolf Ruth, another vet, and on retiring, Ruth senior set out to find the mine. In mid-June 1931 he entered the Superstition Mountains, establishing his camp by a waterhole at Boulder. A visitor to the camp on the next day found Ruth gone, but his boots left in camp.

Widespread searches for months found nothing until, in December, Ruth's skull was found, pierced by two bullet holes, made apparently by an old army pistol. In January 1932 Ruth's skeleton was found, at a considerable distance from his skull. Identified by a silver surgical plate and the pocket contents, the skeleton also had with it a notebook with mysterious jottings which can only refer to the search for the mine. They ended with '*Veni, vidi, vici* (I came, I saw, I conquered) – about 200 feet across from cave', suggesting that Ruth died because he had actually located the mine.

James A. Cravey, a retired photographer, settled in Phoenix in 1946, seeking the mine. In mid-June of 1946 he was helicoptered into the Superstition Mountains, camping in a box canyon with ten days' supplies. Searches began when he had not shown up by early July, but helicopter and ground parties couldn't find him. His camp showed ashes of two days' fires. In February 1948 his headless skeleton was found by two hikers. His skull was located on the following day. The *Arizona Republic*, reporting Cravey's death, said: 'Cravey is the twentieth person known to have lost his life while looking for the fabled lost mine in the Superstitions.'

The practice of taking enemies' heads as evidence is treated in Bourke's book cited above, where he describes seeing as many as seven heads displayed on a parade ground by Apaches. An illustration in *Fighting Indians of the West* shows the Army receiving such a presentation. Perhaps the best evidence that the present narrative is the previously unknown account of Holmes' investigation into the Crosby murder is the fact that this manuscript had been in the hands of my family for a long time before Sims's study of the search for the mine was published, either in America or Britain. If readers believe me in this they will, I think, accept that the present narrative is a genuine work of John H. Watson.

Chapter Eighteen

The highly improbable story of James F. Reavis's attempt to steal the title of Baron of the Colorados and the Territory of Arizona is true as recounted by Sherlock Holmes. It has been told in a number of books (and even filmed with Vincent Price) but a good account of it can be found in Alexander Klein's wonderful anthology *Grand Deception*.

Chapter Nineteen

The oath 'Gordon Bennett!' is believed to refer to James Gordon Bennett, a Scottish emigrant to America who in 1835, founded the *New York Herald*. His journalistic methods were radical and he achieved many worldwide 'scoops', making his name both a household word and a mild expletive. He died in 1872.

Chapter Twenty

Telephone boxes as we know them did not exist in the 1890s, but calls could be placed from 'call offices'. These were maintained by the various telephone companies and contained a number of cubicles with phones. A customer could drop in, pay a fee and have a call connected to one of the cubicles.

It is interesting to note that, in 1894, Mrs Crosby's home was on the telephone and warranted a two-figure number. Bradon must have had a high percentage of wealthy residents! Two-figure (and, in fact, single-figure) numbers survived until the coming of Subscriber Trunk Dialling in the 1960s. My old school had one line whose number in the 1950s was Petersfield 33.

Chapter Twenty-three

A screw jack was a device, much favoured by burglars, for forcing apart the bars that guarded windows. A small cylinder contained the jack mechanism, which was flanked at each end by a saddle-shaped grip. In use, the grips were padded with rag and placed against two adjacent bars. A lever was then inserted in the jack and worked to make it extend, exerting pressure on the two ends. More elaborate varieties had a ratchet mechanism keyed to the jack, so that a longer lever could be applied and pumped, making the effect both much quicker and a great deal more forcible.

Chapter Twenty-five

San Carlos was the principal reservation to which the US Government took the Arizona Apaches. It had a bad reputation with Apaches, despite the efforts of an enlightened agent, John P. Clum. After Washington backed down on General Crook's agreement with the Apaches (see above) all those who surrendered were taken as prisoners, as were scores of innocents who, so far from rebelling against the Army, had served it long and well as scouts. These natives of mountain and desert were shipped to Alabama and Florida, where they sickened and died in large numbers.

It is the case that the red tribes of North America regarded life under the British Crown as considerably preferable to life in the United States. In fact, the Canadian authorities were very anxious not to end up inheriting America's problems. When, in the autumn of 1877 the Sioux Chief Sitting Bull crossed into Canada with three thousand followers, they were permitted to remain but given no assistance. Their repeated requests for reservation land were refused on the basis that they were American citizens (any American lawyer – or any redskin – could have told them that was not true!). A US Army delegation was permitted to cross the frontier under an escort of the Royal Canadian Mounted and try to persuade Sitting Bull to return to America. At first he would not speak to them, telling the Canadians that 'these people tell lies'. He rejected their blandishments but, after a harsh winter in 1880, and in the face of the

Canadian refusals of assistance, he and some two hundred others returned across the frontier in the summer of 1881.

In the foregoing notes I have recited any fact which I believe will assist the reader in deciding whether the present narrative is a genuine production of John H. Watson. I do not pretend that my researches are complete. I am sure there is much more that could be discovered by those with more time available. Nevertheless, for the reasons set out in my Notes, I am as satisfied as I can be that what we have here is a previously unknown record by Dr Watson of another case of Sherlock Holmes.

If I may make a final comment – readers will note that I have not tampered with Watson's use of terms like 'Red Indian', 'Indian' or 'redskin'. They were, after all, the terminology of his day. In my own notes I have eschewed the politically correct 'native Americans'. In the many conferences that took place during the years of the frontier wars the tribal chiefs, without exception, used the term 'Americans' to refer to their white enemies. They did not, apparently, regard themselves as any kind of Americans.